Scion of Scales

The Ironfire Legacy
Book Two

Janeen Ippolito

First edition © 2018 Janeen Ippolito
Second edition © 2021 Janeen Ippolito

All rights reserved. No part of this publication may be reproduced, distributed, or transmitted in any form or by any means, including photocopying, recording, or other electronic or mechanical methods, without the prior written permission of the publisher, except in the case of brief quotations embodied in critical reviews and certain other noncommercial uses permitted by copyright law.

This is a work of fiction. Names, characters, businesses, places, events, and incidents are either the products of the author's imagination or used in a fictitious manner. Any resemblance to actual persons, living or dead, or actual events is purely coincidental.

Editing by Sarah McConahy

Cover Design by Christian Bentulan

To H. L. Burke—save the cat-dragon!

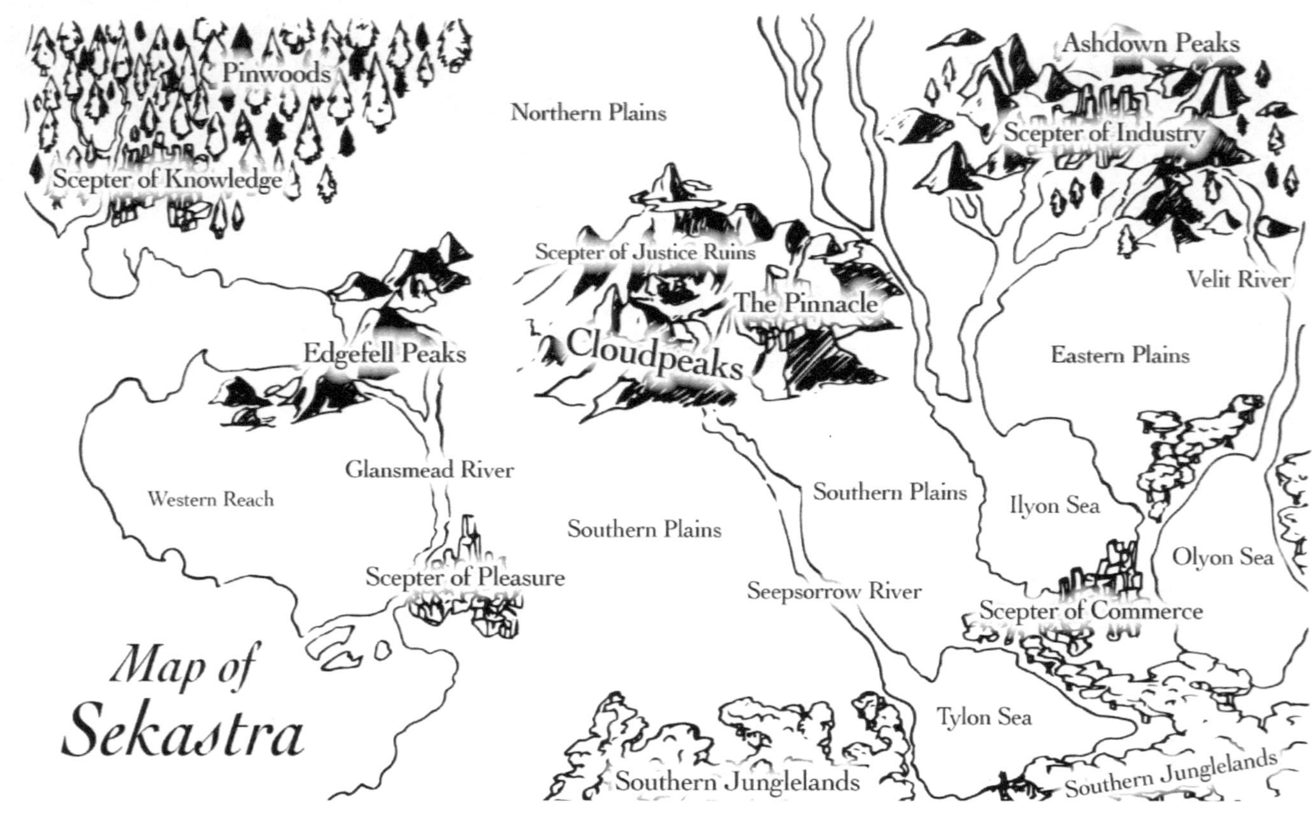
Pinwoods
Northern Plains
Ashdown Peaks
Scepter of Industry
Scepter of Knowledge
Scepter of Justice Ruins
Velit River
The Pinnacle
Edgefell Peaks
Cloudpeaks
Eastern Plains
Glansmead River
Western Reach
Southern Plains
Ilyon Sea
Southern Plains
Olyon Sea
Scepter of Pleasure
Seepsorrow River
Scepter of Commerce
Map of
Sekastra
Tylon Sea
Southern Junglelands
Southern Junglelands

CHAPTER ONE

GETTING A LOVER out of one's hair was the most tedious part of having a lover. Usually, Nula Thredsing would simply leave the room and have her butler sort them out. In this case, however, the lover was her butler.

And that butler, Ferrin, thought she needed more bodyguards. She could tell by the way his frown settled on his features, his thick brown brows coming together over his patrician nose.

"You are aware that this is a dragon, my lady." He adjusted his fitted coat over his lanky frame. "All precautions should be taken, as your parents would have—"

"Am I my parents?" She stopped on the wharf and glared at him. All five feet, eight inches of him, only one inch taller than she was. An unacceptably small height difference. What had she been thinking? She had needed the diversion. "Answer me. Am I a villainous, traitorous conspirator of the Curious Intrigue?"

"No, my lady." He swallowed and pressed his lips together, his fair skin flushing. Broad face, square jaw, strong features, fit body—all fine qualities for the occasional one-night stand. Their last mutually-appreciated dalliance had been eight months ago, long enough that she had forgotten most of what lay under those clothes.

But she had moved on. Soon it would be time to give Ferrin his papers, a suitably glowing recommendation letter, and send him on his way to someone else's employment. He had enough value in his future; from his Talent of keen hearing to his admirable employment record, he would succeed beyond any association with her. Besides, keeping a steady rotation of servants was the only way to ensure one of them didn't get too close and betray her.

It was one of the useful lessons Nula had learned from her parents as she planned to betray them to the Lawless. And Ferrin deserved a good recommendation. He had been an excellent turncoat, assisting her in gathering information to leak to the Lawless, and a suitable addition to the roster of double agents she had recruited over the years. He was personally devoted to the cause, another factor that made him trustworthy enough when the nights grew lonely.

Because they did, once in a while.

She focused on her butler again, sensing his discomfort over the slip-up and perhaps fearing her reprisal. Well, there would be none today. She had more important matters to attend to.

"See that you remember your role." Nula turned on her boot heel and continued down the wharf, veering away from the commercial docks toward the military section. All vessels had been cleared from the Ilyon Sea in order to raise the airship landing pad from beneath the surface of the waves. High Command had many other places for airships to land, but they wanted to make a grand show of this one in honor of the dragon aboard, coming as the first dragon diplomatic envoy to the Scepter of Commerce in twenty years.

Nula smoothed her dark blue corset-coat and the white silk blouse that set off her rich brown skin. It was best to make a good impression, especially as the new Liaison for Dragon Affairs. A temporary title, but one she hoped to make permanent over the next few weeks as the Scepter of Commerce moved to fill the fifth seat on their new ruling council.

Considering that only two weeks ago the city had been outwardly dedicated to the war against dragons, the speed of the transition from military stronghold to fully commercial center was most impressive. But the Scepter of Commerce smelled the possibility of fresh money and more freedoms than High Command had previously allowed. The Lawless needed a representative on the council to ensure that rebel interests would still be respected and to give Kesia and Zephryn a chance to sway the rest of the Congruency to reestablishing the Scepter of Justice.

Who better to fill the position than Nula? After all, Thredsings had a legacy of holding council seats.

Soldiers lined the walkway to the octagonal landing platform, all of them armed to the teeth. Nula nodded to them respectfully as she walked down the raised pathway. At the end stood General Markem, as stiff and craggy as ever in his formal uniform of black brocade waistcoat, burgundy shirt, and black cravat, with a peaked cap perched on his head. She came to a stop next to him, right in front of a line of officers.

"General." She nodded again. "Is everything on schedule?"

"Countess Thredsing. I see you've taken to your new position all too well." He grunted, and the lines on his weathered face deepened. "I still do not answer to you."

Nula raised her eyebrows, swatting lightly at his arm. "Why General, I was only asking a question."

"And I am choosing not to answer what your own eyes can tell you."

He pointed to a growing shape on the horizon. Nula squinted, taking in the details of the airship. It was an older model with a few sails atop it, though the turbines coming out each side made the sails unnecessary. There was some ancient, sentimental reason that airships bearing dragons used sails, and Tiers Sunscaler had made it clear in his sparse missives that certain traditions should be respected.

She hoped he wasn't such a killjoy about everything. Kesia and Zephryn had told her precious little about him. Something about valuing his privacy. How was she supposed to work with him effectively if she didn't know his strengths and weaknesses? What she did know was that this particular dragon was a skilled administrator, had an excellent mind for details, and was completely committed to the reunification of humans and dragons.

Nula had tried to contact Kesia this morning via clipse-mirror in a last-minute effort for additional information. However, Nula had been shut down by Zephryn. He and Kesia were knee-deep in difficulties at the Scepter of Knowledge, and Zephryn didn't want Kesia to be disturbed.

Was it disturbing a friend to check on her welfare for mutual benefit? Nula certainly didn't think so. As a matter of fact—

She turned to her soon-to-be-former butler, who had followed her up the walkway.

"Ferrin, remind me to send a list of additional contacts from the Curious Intrigue over to our Lawless friends in the Scepter of Knowledge. And if there are any favorable leaders in the aristocracy of the Scepter of Knowledge, stand by to bribe them if they cause trouble for Nightstalker and Ironfire."

"Noted, my lady."

With that settled, Nula breathed a sigh of relief and focused again on the airship. It was closer now, the stench of its exhaust fumes mixing with the salty breeze off the Ilyon Sea. There was so much riding on her association with this one dragon. There were other dragons in the Scepter of Commerce, part of the Lawless underground. One of Nula's goals was to convince them to come out of hiding as a way to rebuild relations between the two races. If she was going to make the position of Liaison for Dragon Affairs a legitimate part of the new ruling council, she needed the dragons on her side, and that meant ensuring that Tiers Sunscaler trusted her. Kesia Ironfire counted her a friend, even after Nula had turned her over to High Command, so handling one male dragon would be easy enough.

The wind blew against her tiny braids, whipping them around her face. Nula centered herself firmly on the platform and fixed her eyes on the airship. Landing gear came out of the bottom of the ship, latching on to the keel and fixing everything into place. A gangplank emerged from the side, and sailors scampered down it, setting up the moveable stairs for the dragon dignitary.

At last, the engine shut off and the turbines retracted into the airship. Nula walked closer to the stairs, easily keeping pace with General Markem.

He scowled. "Mind your place, Countess."

"I am." She bared her teeth in a smile. "I am the Liaison for Dragon Affairs, and Tiers Sunscaler is a dragon, which means this is a civil matter, first and foremost, not a military concern. In case you've forgotten, the Scepter of Commerce is in the process of transferring control to the civil authority."

"Yes, but it hasn't happened yet. Even when it does, a strong military presence will still be needed. This Scepter may have declared a cessation of conflict, but there are three other Scepters still supporting the war with their own shipyards and fleets."

"Details, details." Admittedly, these were details Nula wanted to change, but in order to do that, she needed to ally with this dragon.

He was a male, and unattached. From what Nula had managed to glean, dragons only had eyes for their destined embermate, and were notoriously immune to other charms. But she had a little dragon heritage, some ancestor on her mother's side. She might be able to use that, or at least play some kind of kinship card.

The airship captain descended first, her red hair pulled back severely, standing straight and formal in the dark blue and black uniform of airship commanding officers. Behind her loomed the dragon. He had an elegant face with a thatch of black hair, and his tawny skin hid his scales beneath a human facade. Calm golden eyes studied everything around him critically, and the effortless way he carried himself hinted at the warrior training all dragons received.

Handsome, but not exceptional. Nula had seen many attractive individuals in her time. Yet she couldn't help but give him another once-over, noticing the way the tailored black pants, crisp emerald shirt, and black vest enhanced his toned figure.

Foolish. There would be no taking this dragon as a lover. He was destined for some elusive embermate. A female of his own kind.

For some reason, she wanted to rip the limbs off this theoretical female.

Sunscaler's eyes caught hers and narrowed. One blink. Two. Then his gaze darted away, and his jaw clenched.

Nula's face flushed, and she swallowed, tasting his value. An overwhelming flavor of gold, warm and smooth and as brilliant as his eyes. He was even more valuable than the dragon prince Zephryn Nightstalker, which made as little sense as the irresistible pull of his mouth and skin.

Enough! Perhaps she should have one last night with Ferrin before sending him on his way. A farewell tangle in the sheets for old time's sake. Or better yet, perhaps find a nameless gentleman for a tryst. Something to release the tension from her, a ridiculous tension that would find no release in a dragon.

Utterly irrational.

"Good day, Sunscaler," Markem rumbled next to her. "You are certain there is no other title we should call you?"

"None is needed." The dragon's voice was lighter and less assuming than Zephryn's, and there was a quiet but certain cadence to his dragon resonance. Very pleasing—not that it mattered. "If you must, consider me another count. That should suffice."

A count. He just named himself a count as if it were a meaningless trifle. Annoyance filled Nula. She might have been born a countess, but with parents like hers, that had been no guarantee of living to enjoy the title. After joining the Lawless, she had fought hard to gain power and respect. Tiers owned his strength as if it were nothing. Of course he did. After all, he was a fire-breathing dragon barely contained in human form. How typical for those with innate power to value it so little.

That killed any interest she had in the dragon. Entirely. Never mind his value. He would be merely Sunscaler in her mind.

The dragon turned toward her. "You are Countess Nula Thredsing, I presume?"

She nodded and flashed him a smile. "Indeed. Your official liaison to the Scepter of Commerce. I would have been happy to introduce myself sooner over clipse-mirror."

"There was no time."

Nula tsked. "Yes, everyone here has time-consuming duties. Including the crown prince and princess of dragons. Kesia and Zephryn have told me as much over clipse-mirrors."

Sunscaler's eyes flashed a deeper gold, clearly annoyed. "Their graces may do as they wish. As can I."

A deeper vibrato undergirded his tone, almost threatening. Nula stiffened. "You may find in the Scepter of Commerce that doing as you wish has consequences. Particularly when it concerns others who are trying to assist you."

"Others who are trying to assist themselves through me, you mean." His lips twitched. "Certainly not you, of course, Countess Thredsing."

General Markem cleared his throat, though it sounded suspiciously like laughter. Behind her, Ferrin was even less discreet.

She would definitely send him on his way today.

"Ambition is my favorite accessory. Especially when no one else can do the job as well as I can." Nula raised her eyebrows. "Now, let's clear the platform. The ship needs to be checked over, and there are many people eager to meet you."

"I'm sure." Was that a twinge of distaste in his eyes?

Nula clenched her jaw. He was entering her city, awarded a title purely for his race and power, and had the nerve to be annoyed by a simple meeting with leading officials? How useless was he?

Still, she had to be polite.

She flashed him another smile. "Did you have a safe flight?"

"Obviously." He shrugged, then paused. "My apologies. Human small talk is still cumbersome."

"But a very useful skill to master. How did you become a diplomat with such a deficiency?"

"Wartime makes strange bedfellows of us all. Most strange."

Sunscaler was staring at her as if she were an odd creature that he didn't know how to approach. Nula rolled her eyes. Being uncouth around her was one matter, but they would have to work together. She didn't need an incompetent dragon ruining her machinations with his gawking expressions.

She lowered her voice. "A bit of advice, *Count* Sunscaler: when among humans, try to contain your amazement at our grounded ways. It will make your life, and mine, a lot easier."

"Noted." His breath was warm and faintly tinged with ash. "A returning bit of advice, Countess Thredsing."

"Yes?"

"You should hold your breath."

A hideous shriek pierced the air, followed by a roar louder and deeper than an airship turbine. Flames and smoke filled the sky.

Sunscaler lunged at her, grabbed her close—and leaped into the Ilyon Sea.

Chapter Two

TIERS ALREADY LOVED the incorrigible woman. He must. Otherwise, he wouldn't have jumped into the worst place possible in order to protect her—a large body of water.

Yet, as he held her close, treading water and tasting the flames and ash in the air, he knew there had been no other choice. Countess Thredsing could not be allowed to die. No harm would come to her as long as he lived—and his own life would be forfeit to ensure her survival.

His throat heated.

Fewmets. This couldn't have happened at a worse time.

She struggled in his arms, blinking away the water that ran down her forehead into her eyes. The sounds of cannons and gunfire drowned out all other noise, including Countess Thredsing's words, which undoubtedly concerned why he treaded water with her in his arms.

"You were in danger! *Dragons!*"

She winced. Yes, his voice was loud. But that was the only way Tiers could hear it. Her full lips parted in a grimace, and she shouted back, "*You* are in danger if you keep holding me."

Such gratitude. More cannon fire boomed overhead, and dragon flames singed the air. He sighed. Under normal circumstances, he would be in the sky, attacking the invaders. But Countess Thredsing took priority, even if she didn't understand why. Which, clearly, she did not.

"Can you swim?"

At that moment, another blast of cannons seared the air. She shook her head, confusion evident in her clear gray eyes. Blast. She couldn't hear him.

She had such beautiful eyes. Intelligent and calculating as a dragon's, but lit with fiery passion, like brilliant stars against her velvet skin. Instinctively, he freed one hand and stroked the edge of her cheekbone up to the thin decorative rod that pierced the bridge of her nose. The contact sent a pulse of warmth through his fingers. <If only you could sense what we have.>

Her eyes widened. <What do you mean?>

Shock rippled through him. Tiers quickly filed it away and focused on more important matters. <You can hear me? Can you swim?>

<Yes. You need to get up there and stop them!>

<I know.> He stroked her cheek one last time. <We will discuss this later.>

Nula glared at him with a ferocity that took his breath away. <You're damn right we will.>

Tiers pulled away and the connection broke. Immediately a part of him felt alone in a way he'd never realized was possible, for he'd never had anyone else so close to his heart.

His heart. She was human. Could their hearts even be properly joined? How was this possible?

Think later. Act now.

He shifted, and the waves parted around him as his mass grew and scales replaced skin. With a grunt of effort, Tiers forced himself free of the distasteful, clinging water and rose into the sky, his wings free at last.

Cannon fire shot past his left shoulder. He wheeled around and ducked, curving through the air. If Nula was as intelligent as her demeanor suggested, she would inform High Command to avoid shooting at him.

He took in the scene. Two dragons against the weaponry secured in the wharf. The human's artillery was extensive, but it lacked the mobility of dragons. From the flames and smoke streaming from several buildings and public areas, he knew the dragons had realized this.

Tiers growled and zeroed in on the nearest dragon. Slender and glimmering deep orange, its hind end turned toward him. Foolish warrior, distracted in the heat of attack. He blasted a warning shot of flame at its tail. <Leave. Now.>

The dragon screeched and banked sharply to the left, swooping around to face him. Something in the shriek seemed familiar. <You and who else, Tiers Sunscaler? I think we have you nicely cornered.>

The voice brought the enemy dragon's skin form to mind. Brown hair threaded with orange. Green eyes glinting with self-assurance and levity.

Tiers's heart sank into his stomach. It had been ten years. Of all the people the Pinnacle could have sent, it had to be his closest friend, the one who had broken his heart. Grief and anger blurred his eyes. He dodged, barely avoiding another burst of flame.

It couldn't be.

<Yaron? Yaron Flamestriker?>

<Traitor.> The other dragon spat a flame of fire. <Always a traitor. Even now, you come to their docks in skin form, pandering to their peace treaties. Have you still not seen reason? I thought you

had more backbone than that.>

Anger shuddered through Tiers's wings as he dodged another blast of fire. <Are you still consumed with falsehoods from the Pinnacle? I thought you were smarter than that.>

<I'm not the dragon who betrayed their own kind.>

<The war isn't real!>

Flames singed his tail. Tiers whirled around to see a slender female dragon, scales glimmering indigo and her dark eyes glowing with fire and rage. <Saying it again doesn't make it true. Take care with my fleetwing, Tiers Sunscaler.>

<Jylle Steelslicer.> The embermate his old tactical partner had found after they had parted ways. Tiers growled. She had been the final straw that swayed Yaron to complete devotion to the Pinnacle and its lies. Embermates—or fleetwings, as the Pinnacle insisted on calling them—were marked by a strong alignment of values and emotional synchronization, not merely physical attraction.

Which had interesting implications for Tiers's own pull to Nula Thredsing. Implications that would have to be dealt with later.

He snorted out a stream of smoke and dove at Jylle, leaving Yaron alone in the sky. Hopefully that would be sufficient for the human military to do their job.

A second later, cannon fire blasted through the air. Yaron's ferocious screech and the sudden scent of dragon blood indicated a hit. The orange dragon darted away, his flight hindered by the blow to his wing.

<You'll pay for this, Sunscaler.> Jylle fixed him with a final glare before flying after her wounded fleetwing. She had no choice. His pain was her own, and there could be no separation.

Tiers started after them, then paused and glanced down. Nula Thredsing was a tiny figure below, safe on the edge of the dock.

But he had to ensure her protection above all else, which meant the fight could not be continued. Besides, Jylle would be twice as fierce in defense of her embermate, and Yaron couldn't go far with a broken wing. Better to land and finish with the diplomatic affairs. Doubtless the humans would be upset about the attack.

Tiers certainly was.

He descended toward the Ilyon Sea, shifting into skin form and landing in the water. Tiers grit his teeth against the cold and swam to the edge of the dock. Unpleasant liquid. With the danger over, being immersed in the sea made his skin crawl. He almost pulled himself out onto the dock before remembering that humans had a strong taboo about public nudity. Foolish of them. If certain body parts offended them so much, why could they not simply avert their eyes?

Still, he remained in the water. And as he took in Nula Thredsing's form, he amended the thought. *He* was the one having trouble averting his eyes due to the still-wet clothes clinging to her figure. Physical attraction was meant to be with an embermate, according to his parents and other mated dragons Tiers had observed in the Lawless.

An embermate who was a human. This would complicate matters. Perhaps discretion would be the wiser choice.

The countess's pale gray eyes lighted on him and narrowed. She threw a towel and a set of clothing in his direction, and they fell to the dock in front of him. "We need to leave. Now. Before any more Flamers show up."

"I agree." Yes, withholding information about their embermate bond was definitely wiser for now. She hardly seemed aware of anything other than her own fury. Tiers shared her anger. The only reason his throat wasn't literally on fire was because of the water drenching his skin.

She turned away, as did the others around her. Tiers quickly climbed up on the dock, dried himself, and put on the clothes. A military uniform, ill-fitting compared to the attire he had stowed on the ship, clothing that was likely shredded in the depths of the Ilyon Sea. The pant hems reached just above his ankles, the shirt cuffs came halfway down his forearms, and the shoes were unwearable. Annoyance flitted through him. So much for making a strong first impression.

"You can turn around."

Nula Thredsing twisted to face him. She looked him over, and her jaw clenched. "Where are the shoes?"

He offered them to her. "They're too small for my feet."

"Ah. Perfect." Her rich voice cut each word into syllables like a knife. "Come on, *Count* Sunscaler. Before this day gets any worse."

She whirled and strode down the pavement, every inch a confident woman, her posture radiating strength and purpose. He found himself eyeing the area where her back met her legs.

Zephryn must have made a mistake when he warned Tiers about Nula Thredsing. She seemed entirely suited for her role in the Lawless. Then again, Zephryn was equally stubborn in his own way, which had certainly clashed with the strong-willed countess. She was the sort that could make trouble.

Trouble that was currently walking away from him on the wharf. He began following her, keeping his pace sure and measured. Dragons had no need to chase after anyone, and he preferred the silence to better collect his thoughts.

Besides, the view was pleasant from this angle.

Far more pleasant than knowing his old tactical partner had been sent to ruin Tiers's mission.

And possibly the new alliance with the humans as well.

CHAPTER THREE

HER FUTURE WAS out to get her. Nula was certain of this. Even though her abilities to read value and potential didn't extend to herself, this entire scenario confirmed her suspicions.

She stared out the window of the groundcar, taking in the tall claymesh buildings of the Scepter of Commerce, brilliant with inlaid mosaics. She tried to ignore the clammy wetness of her clothing and the water that still dripped from her tiny braids. Her fingers picked at the edges of her jacket.

She and her future were old adversaries. So far, Nula had won every battle. Whoever controlled the future—Bonilus, the All-Maker, or whatever other deity—their regard for her seemed highly fickle. But she still came through stronger.

This was simply another challenge.

"Where are we going?"

She sighed. The dragon was talking again. Ferrin had taken the second car back to the mansion to collect his papers, having been dismissed from her service according to plan. This left Nula alone with Sunscaler, who, despite his attractive face, looked like a fool in the cast-off military uniform. And to top it all off, his feet were bare going into an important council meeting. She was glad she'd refused a change of clothing. Her attire might be wet, but at least she was still appropriate for high-level politics.

She managed to summon a small smile. "We're on our way to the Central Market."

Sunscaler's golden eyes glinted. "Ah, yes. High Command headquarters, currently being transferred to the ruling council."

"Yes." If he knew, why did he ask her? She flicked a braid of hair over her shoulder in annoyance. It didn't matter. If he wanted conversation, she'd make sure it was useful. "While we are there, follow my lead. The ruling council is newly-formed and skittish. They need to be handled carefully to ensure they make the appropriate decisions."

"Such as endorsing your appointment as Liaison for Dragon Affairs? Perhaps with an appointment to the council itself?"

Her eyebrows raised. "How did you know my position was temporary?"

Sunscaler smirked, his light voice edged with intelligence. "You are not the only one whose business it is to know everything and ensure everything runs properly. I do my own research."

"I prefer to hire others to do my research and use my mind for more worthwhile things."

"Such as controlling people?"

Nula rolled her eyes. She should be playing a stronger role as helpful cohort and liaison, but something about the dragon's quiet, knowing attitude made her skin prickle and undid her smooth words. "Yes. It's called leadership. I control them because someone has to, and I'm good at it, despite what you may have heard about me. I get matters accomplished."

A smile spread across his face, and his voice deepened with more of that famed dragon resonance. "I'm sure. You don't need to worry about me intruding on your plans. I've found that I am more effective when people underestimate me. Feel free to control others as you wish."

"As if I need your permission." Nula tsked.

Sunscaler leaned forward, his hand resting next to hers. Their skin barely touched, but warmth emanated from the slight contact. "You are welcome to argue otherwise, if you think that would be a good use of your incredibly valuable time."

"That is for me to decide."

"Of course it is." His smile widened.

Nula's lips parted, and her chest tightened. The dragon continued to mock her, as if making a private joke! Her skin prickled in exasperation, and the sensation turned into a curious heat that pressed against her skin. It was more than arousal. It felt as if something were trying to surface from within her, something wild that she had no chance of controlling. Nor did she entirely want to. Her Talent was certain this man was worth more than gold, but it hadn't seen fit to indicate *why*.

"Who are you?" The words came out softer than she intended. "How did you speak inside my mind when we were in the water? What are you doing to me?"

At that moment, the car stopped in front of the Central Market. Tiers pulled away from her, his expression reserved and professional. "Count Tiers Sunscaler, dragon diplomat to the Scepter of Commerce. At your service."

"Yes, but—" The driver opened her door. Nula pursed her lips and brushed off her suit, as if attempting to remove the strange effect Sunscaler had on her.

Absurd. She was supposed to be disarming him at her convenience, not the other way around. And that would only be for the purposes of good business communication. She dare not risk anything more than a purely professional situation until she could understand and counteract him.

Not that she wanted him anyway.

As for the incident in the water, maybe Sunscaler had spoken aloud, and she had only imagined his mind touching hers. It had been an intense situation. Her senses may have been playing tricks.

"Follow me, Count Sunscaler."

Nula got out of the car. It was better to focus on the meeting ahead and ensure it spun in her favor. And Sunscaler's as well. After all, she was responsible for keeping track of him. He might have some indefinable allure, possibly due to her own dragon heritage, but he was still new to the city.

It would be up to her to handle everything. Including the fiasco at the wharf.

Nula Thredsing was more than trouble. She was *in* trouble. Her response to the embermate pull was too unpredictable, and right now enough unpredictable things had happened.

The sense of foreboding sank deep into Tiers's heart as he followed her across the plaza with its three fountains and veered around to a side entrance. She seemed utterly composed, pressing her palm to a bioelectric scanner embedded in the glimmering gold and silver tiles of the massive edifice. A door slid aside, revealing a long hallway with smooth gray claymesh on all sides.

He tilted his head. "A secret entrance?"

"Main entrances are for grand displays or visitors who don't know any better." She laughed a little as she continued walking.

"At least in my case."

"I see."

The fingers of Nula Thredsing's right hand clenched, then unclenched. A response to the embermate bond, or some other anxiety? Perhaps both? For dragons, the knowledge of an embermate was instantaneous, and the urge to connect with the other equally rapid. In the case of some, such as Kesia and Zephryn, the realization of the bond could occur before setting eyes on each other.

But, according to her dossier, Nula Thredsing was human with dragon ancestry. How much dragon DNA did she have? How would it react? He needed to do more research before attempting to initiate any contact. She was already agitated. Provoking her could make things worse or cause her harm.

A sigh escaped him as they turned down another hallway. A pity. It was fun provoking Nula, to see her smile back in challenge, her teeth gleaming white against her deep, smooth brown skin.

Skin he dearly wanted to touch again.

"Is there something wrong, Count Sunscaler?"

Had he stopped walking? Yes, the irritated flash in her clear gray eyes made that obvious. Tiers blinked and shook his head, then started walking again. "Perhaps the events of the day are beginning to take their toll."

"Ah, yes." She made another tsking sound. "Well, it will get worse before it gets better. There is no point in delaying. The sooner we arrive, the sooner we can manage the situation."

Tiers advanced until he walked abreast of her. Curiosity loosened his tongue. "Did you say 'we'?"

"You are the dragon diplomat, so you should answer in some capacity. But as the official liaison, the greater burden of discussion will fall on my shoulders." Nula shook her head in exasperation. "I can't believe I'm appearing before political powers in a soaked suit with a barefoot foreign politician."

"Just say it's a dragon custom. Humans tend to believe that."

"Is it?" She raised her eyebrows.

He shrugged. "When meeting in skin form, we tend to be less formally dressed than humans. Ostentatious clothing is an unnecessary distraction."

Nula Thredsing gave a chuckle, this one light and unburdened by anxiety. "It does sound more comfortable, but I prefer to use every tool at my disposal, especially when it has positive effects."

"Among dragons, you wouldn't need excessive clothing. Your presence alone would command a room." Which was likely one reason why Zephryn disliked her. The crown prince still had much to learn about engaging others as a leader.

She flashed him a smile. "I'm glad to hear that, considering how I need to prove to the council that Liaison for Dragon Affairs should be a permanent position."

"I have no doubt you will."

Nula Thredsing gave him a sharp look, as if testing the truth of his words. Tiers stared back innocently with a faint smile, the one that seemed to unnerve her.

Provoking her a little couldn't do any harm.

They turned a corner and entered a large semicircular room. On one side, the curving wall was paned with glass. Sunlight flooded across the floor, warming the tiles beneath Tiers's feet. On the other side stood a long table of polished metal with five seats behind it. Four of the chairs were occupied by two men and two women, their expressions a spectrum of thoughtful and perturbed.

The fifth seat was empty.

Nula Thredsing's gaze lingered on it. Her seat. Or it would

be, once they approved her role. Tiers caught a fleeting glimpse of wistfulness and determination on her face before it was replaced by her usual calculating politeness.

She gave a half-bow. "Grand Counts and Countesses, I'm afraid I have disturbing news."

A pale woman with piercing blue eyes made a small gesture with a thin hand. Grand Countess Glimmerly. "Go on, Countess Thredsing. We have already been informed of such by General Markem." The grand countess gestured to a bronze wireless commer on her desk. "Two dragons attacked the airship *Swift Arrow* as it was docked by the Ilyon Sea. Count Sunscaler protected you, then launched himself into the air to provide support to the soldiers who mounted a cannon defense against the invading dragons. What can you or Count Sunscaler add to this existing knowledge?"

Tiers's mind raced. Telling them of his personal connection to Yaron Flamestriker wasn't an option, but there were other details he could share. "The male dragon, Yaron Flamestriker, is an ardent supporter of the Pinnacle. At one time, he was being groomed as a double agent, but he chose to oppose the resistance. He now has a fleetwing, an embermate, who shares his fervor. I can't say for certain, but given the proximity to my arrival, I speculate that they are committed to disrupting the dragon-human reconciliation ceremony next week by any means necessary."

"Which means we must oppose them by any means necessary." Nula Thredsing's words were strong and firm. "Any sign of backing down will prove to the Curious Intrigue and the Pinnacle that attacks like these are effective."

A balding man at the end of the table cleared his throat and rubbed his wrinkled hands together. Grand Count Fawson. "At the same time, Countess Thredsing, the reconciliation ceremony is a public event. If the dragon attacks were to succeed, the fallout could be catastrophic, particularly with regard to civilian casualties."

"Agreed," said the second man behind the table. He was younger with light brown skin and thick eyebrows that twitched as he spoke. Grand Count Petrellin. "We must judge this situation carefully and inform the authorities to track down this dragon pair as quickly as possible."

Which would undoubtedly lead to their interrogation in Tiers's presence. No doubt every word out of Yaron's and Jylle's mouths would expose his role as a double agent. It would be a diplomatic nightmare, since he had every interest in keeping that part of his job a secret.

His pulse quickened, and smoke filled his mouth. He swallowed it down and kept his voice measured. "That will be unnecessary, Grand Counts and Countesses. I am certain that Countess Thredsing and I can locate the perpetrators within the week and deliver them to you with minimal disturbance. Though they are dragons, one is injured and will need to find shelter in a safe place somewhere in the city. There are rumors of a secret laboratory and healing facility that the Lawless have yet to locate. This incident gives us a chance to find this hideout and capture their base of operations. And we will."

Grand Countess Glimmerly raised her eyebrows. "Are you so certain?"

"Yes." Nula Thredsing's voice rang with confidence. "And when we deliver them into your hands, with suitable assistance from the authorities as required, that will be reason enough to confirm the position of Liaison for Dragon Affairs to the final council seat."

Fire flared within Tiers for an entirely different reason, and he fought the grin that threatened to spread across his face. Nula

Thredsing was indomitable, indeed. The glances between council members only served to prove her power.

At last, the remaining woman, Grand Countess Damsted, nodded, her loose curls bouncing on her plump, honey-colored shoulders. "Yes. If you bring in these two dragons before the time of the reconciliation ceremony, then you, Countess Nula Thredsing, will be elevated to the role of Grand Countess and be given the rights and responsibilities of a full-term council member."

"Agreed." Nula Thredsing's eyes gleamed in anticipation. "Good day, Grand Counts and Countesses."

Grand Count Fawson nodded. "Good day. This council meeting is adjourned."

She gave another half-bow and left the room, Tiers keeping pace with her and trying to resist the urge to take her in his arms and kiss her for the strength and resolve she had showed.

Reserve. Patience. He needed to know more before any additional contact was made.

Nula Thredsing had other ideas. As soon as they exited the Central Market, she turned and grabbed his arm, fixing him with a glare.

"You are a dragon of many secrets. Tell me, Count Sunscaler, what else are you keeping from me?"

<That knowledge must wait until later.>

She raised her eyebrows, then pursed her lips. "Oh, must it?"

Surprise burned through Tiers. Fewmets! How had she—the physical contact. It enabled dragon mindspeak between them.

Tiers pulled out of her grasp and began walking toward the groundcar. "Despite what you've been led to believe, Countess, you are not entitled to answers for every single question."

He stepped inside the groundcar. She followed, giving directions to the driver, then fixed him with another one of her fierce, beguiling smiles.

"My dear Count Sunscaler, but I most certainly am."

Fire flamed in his throat.

This woman would be the end of him.

CHAPTER FOUR

UNTIL THIS MOMENT, Nula had never imagined tolerating a man so stubborn. She usually found a way to manage difficult men or gave up and moved on to more likely prospects, as she had with Zephryn Nightstalker at the gala a few weeks ago.

But Nightstalker hadn't spoken to her using dragon mind-speak. Sunscaler had. And he had a very confusing effect on her, particularly in close proximity.

She was getting answers before they continued working together, even though Sunscaler seemed equally determined not to give them to her. He stared resolutely out the window, body turned away from her.

She exhaled shortly in disbelief. Silence? Did he really think that would work? Nula leaned back against the seat. He would talk.

He just needed the right provocation.

"You have a pleasant mental voice. Nearly as pleasant as your actual one, with that lovely resonance."

Sunscaler didn't move. Hmm. Flattery wasn't going to work. Time for another tactic.

"Of course, it's well known that dragons are attractive in general. Something about your kind luring airship sailors to their deaths and stealing away princesses for nefarious purposes."

The dragon scowled, and a few golden scales glinted across his forehead. Losing control of his skin form? He seemed to prefer accuracy to old wives' tales. So did she, though the myths were hilarious when bandied about over drinks.

Maybe push just a little further.

"Still, even the official Liaison for Dragon Affairs can't be too careful," Nula added. "I wouldn't want you stealing me away. This groundcar will drop you off at your quarters in the diplomats' tower. We can reconvene later for a meal and further notes."

Sunscaler turned toward her abruptly, his golden eyes flaring with orange fire. "Unacceptable. I'll join you at your house."

"Why? The diplomat accommodations are excellent. And it seems you prefer your own thoughts and space, which I can appreciate."

Her stomach twisted with the words. Truth be told, her own mansion had grown empty as the Lawless had come to the forefront in the Scepter of Commerce. Many of the agents under her had requested positions that required less deception and fewer underhanded tactics. Nula couldn't blame them; she was trying to leave much of that behind herself.

She simply had greater ambitions than becoming a shopkeeper or marrying a lover.

Nula added, "I am perfectly fine in solitude, and I do not need company."

Sunscaler was staring at her intently, as if trying to read her soul. "You don't mean that."

"Oh? And why would you say that?"

He leaned forward, his voice lowering. "You are as lonely as I am."

Her mouth dropped open. How did he know that? “And still you keep talking without a single ounce of proof that I am lonely.”

“Which is no different than you speaking of ancient, slanderous stories about the misdeeds of old dragons.”

“Are you so sure they are all slanderous?”

Sunscaler smirked. “Oh, dragons are certainly capable of misdeeds—”

Suddenly, the vehicle swerved to the left, the driver spewing a mouthful of colorful curses. The motion threw Nula into Sunscaler’s arms, where he caught her awkwardly, her forehead pressed into his chest. She pushed away, gripping his shoulders for balance. His hands closed over hers, and as she looked up, in his expression was the same protectiveness she’d seen before he swept her into the water.

As if she were the most important person in the world.

<You are.>

The words floated into her mind with such certainty that it stirred a soft and fragile hope in her heart. She almost found herself agreeing and responding in kind. Almost. <What’s happening between us?>

The car swerved sharply in the opposite direction, skidding into the curb with a crunch. The driver swore a few more vulgar phrases and turned off the engine.

Nula found herself held securely in Sunscaler’s arms again, breathing in the scent of flame and ash even as his mind whispered to hers, <We’re destined.>

Destined? That could only mean—no. It wasn’t possible.

The driver looked through the divider between the front and back seats. “I’m sorry, my lady. My lord. I don’t usually go off like that, but that little monster came out of nowhere. It almost seemed to be attacking the car!"

Nula pulled out of Sunscaler's arms once more, trying to restore whatever shreds of dignity she had left from this unfortunate day. She pressed down her braids and stared directly at the driver. "A monster, you say?"

"Something like that! Maybe it escaped from those labs the Lawless are shutting down." The driver glanced in the oval, bronze-lined rearview mirror. "It's flat on the ground behind us now."

"Well then, we should investigate."

"My lady, I don't think that's a good idea."

"I don't care." Rude, perhaps, but she had already been attacked by dragons today. She couldn't expect any worse at the hands of an escaped laboratory creature. Nula already wasn't getting answers from Sunscaler on something increasingly compelling and mysterious. She did not feel like dealing with another mystery.

Besides, the poor creature could be injured. Or want to injure them. She had a sidearm at her waist and years of experience using it. Either way, she was prepared.

Nula opened the door and exited the groundcar. On the other side, Sunscaler did the same, his expression guarded. She raised her eyebrows. "Are you scared of the monster, Count Sunscaler?"

"Hardly. I am a dragon, Countess Thredsing." He smiled slightly, matching her stride as they approached the creature sprawled on the pavement behind them.

A strangled mewl emerged from the lump of short, orange fur and pockmarked scales. Nula slowed her pace, curiosity overtaking her irritation. "What is it?"

Sunscaler frowned. "Some kind of dragon? A cliff lizard, perhaps. They have wings."

"Yes, but not fur."

The creature pulled itself up from the ground with jerky, hesitant movements. It sat about a foot tall with a long, scaly golden tail that came to a pointed tip. Its slit-pupiled green eyes were flecked with gold, and its pointed ears twitched curiously. The flat nose wrinkled, flicking golden whiskers above a fanged mouth. Its body was covered with short orange fur interspersed with golden speckles, and two wings sprouted from its back, each one three feet long.

The beast opened its mouth and gave another broken mewl. Blood dripped down over its face. Nula's heart twisted. It was just a stupid beast doing a stupid thing, but she knelt and reached out her hands. Somehow, she felt the creature wouldn't harm her.

"Come here."

The cat-dragon stared at her, then glared at Sunscaler. Nula chuckled. Seemed like she and the wounded beast held the same opinion about the dragon.

"Countess Thredsing, are you sure this is a good idea?"

"No." She focused on the cat-dragon. "But I'm doing it anyway. What can I say? We wounded, vicious creatures have to stick together."

Wounded? Nula could have swallowed her tongue. Hopefully the thick sarcasm hid the truth.

Slowly, the cat-dragon limped over to her outstretched arms. It favored its bloodied left paw. That explained the constant wing extension; it was trying to keep its balance. One more step and the cat-dragon collapsed into her arms with a choked mewl. She ran her fingers over its fine, short coat. *His* fine, short coat.

A faint, growly purr emanated from the creature, causing Nula's muscles to relax. She continued stroking the cat-dragon. Where had it come from? The driver was right: the Lawless had shut down the secret laboratories and confiscated or killed all experiments.

The cat-dragon had to have come from somewhere else.

Sunscaler knelt next to her. She glanced at him to see a wry look on his face. "He's coming home with us to your house, isn't he?"

"Yes, he is." The dragon still hadn't answered her questions about the mindspeak or his reluctance to stay in the diplomat quarters, but if he came with her, Nula would have more opportunities to question him.

A thought struck her, and she turned to Sunscaler. "The healing facility you mentioned to the council, the one the Curious Intrigue has in the city. Do you think it could have a laboratory where they are experimenting on animals?"

"That is a strong possibility." Sunscaler scratched the cat-dragon behind the ear. "Do you think this little monster escaped from there?"

She stood, carefully cradling the cat-dragon in her arms. "I think it's a *very* strong possibility." She turned toward the car. The cat-dragon started hissing, his short fur standing on end.

Nula chuckled and rubbed his head reassuringly. "Against cars? Very well."

She walked over to the groundcar and spoke a few words to the driver, then began walking down the sidewalk.

Sunscaler snorted. "Let me guess: follow you?"

"If you want to get to my house? Yes, if your bare feet can stand it. Otherwise, you can take the car."

"Shoes are a human invention. I'll manage."

Tiers Sunscaler fell into step beside her. Naturally. Easily. His presence gave her a sense of relief somehow, while simultaneously sending shivers through her. She tried not to think about it too much. There were more important matters at stake.

Such as finding this secret healing facility.

And saving the cat-dragon.

CHAPTER FIVE

COUNTESS NULA THREDSING lived in a very impressive cave. She called it a mansion. He knew that word, of course, but the three stories of sculpted claymesh embedded with patterns of steel and silver made him catch his breath and maintain that despite its grandeur, it was still a cave. Not as impressive as the great towers and caverns of old, but an accomplishment nonetheless. Worthy of any dragon.

Or part dragon. Although Tiers had yet to confirm such with the woman, only a human with significant dragon blood could be the embermate of a dragon.

Countess Thredsing paused in the immense doorway, glancing over her shoulder. Her pale gray eyes glinted with equal parts pride and impatience. "If you're done gawking, will you come inside?"

"Certainly."

He followed her through a large, open hall flanked with square pillars the same shade as her eyes. The walls glittered with mirror and silver mosaics, and the room was rimmed with balconies around the second and third floors. The tile floor was cool and firm beneath his feet. It would be a secure place to rest for a night. Particularly with her nearby.

His embermate.

Tiers sighed. There was no telling how long Countess Thredsing would remain distracted from her persistent questions.

Part of him dreaded her forwardness. The rest of him found it flattering and completely fitting. Her words heated his desire to argue back, to challenge her with words until matters became more physical and intimate, and they claimed each other once and for all.

He clenched his fist. Damn dragon instincts. They would not rule him now. They had a far more important mission to accomplish.

Countess Thredsing strode to a metal-lined staircase at the end of the hall, still holding the cat-dragon close. "The first floor is official business for the Lawless. We won't bother them with this. As it stands, I'll be relying on whatever medical knowledge you have to bandage him up."

Tiers caught up with her and they began ascending the stairs. "What of your ever-present right hand? The grimacing human?"

She shot him an annoyed look. "Don't you remember? I dismissed him permanently when we left the docks."

He nodded in satisfaction. "I know you sent him away. I didn't know it was final."

"Very final. By now he will have picked up his work papers and recommendation and begun to make an honest life for himself."

"Good." The fact that the other male, evidently close to Countess Thredsing, had been released from her service, settled something deep and primal within Tiers. Of all the times to grow territorial, this had to be one of the worst. He sighed a stream of smoke as they reached the top of the stairs. "I assume you have a medical kit?"

"Oh, yes. And I even know how to use it. Well, half of it. With your help."

"How can you be sure I'll be helpful?"

Countess Thredsing shrugged, leading them through an arched doorway on their right. "The cat-dragon dies, otherwise. You wouldn't want that on your conscience, right?"

Her last words came out as a threatening purr. Gundeaths! How alluring her spicy brown skin was, how velvety-soft her hair.

The cat-dragon gave a pitiful mewl, clearing all other thoughts from Tiers's mind and pinching his heart. He nodded. "I know field medicine. We should be able to care for him."

"Good."

They entered a room with a long table of dark polished wood lined with six chairs. Pale blue and white mosaics covered the top half of the walls, giving the illusion of flight. From waist-level down, dark wood cabinets filled the remainder of the space.

Countess Thredsing untangled the cat-dragon from her arms and set him on the table. He gave a yowl and clawed at the surface.

"Go right ahead. There are plenty of scratches already there." Countess Thredsing smirked and scratched behind the animal's right ear, calming him. Then she gestured toward Tiers. "Check the cabinets for a medkit."

Tiers quickly found a dented bronze case with a unicorn horn on the cover. He pulled it out and set it on the table over a particularly large gouge in the gleaming brown wood. Unusual for the sophisticated house. "Why are there scratches on the table?"

Countess Thredsing shrugged. "My parents often made exchanges of rare and valuable objects or chemicals here. The table took the brunt. On to more important matters. There should be gauze and disinfectant cream in the kit. I'll distract the beast, and you take care of it."

"Always giving orders, hmm?" Tiers opened the kit and pulled out a clean cloth and disinfectant liquid. He began wiping the gash on the cat-dragon's head, drawing a hiss and a yowl from its fanged mouth.

"Only when I have the best ideas. If you'd like, I could wait until we stare at each other awkwardly and decide who gets to go first." Countess Thredsing rolled her eyes. "So, since we're here, why did you refuse the diplomat quarters? And why do I hear your voice in my mind sometimes?"

Fewmets. Still determined to get answers before he had any satisfactory ones to give her.

"Since you have the best ideas, why don't you tell me what you think?" Tiers focused on applying the ointment. Fortunately, the cat-dragon didn't require stitches. Dragon tech used scale-screen to seal wounds. With the cat-dragon having both fur and scales, Tiers wouldn't have been sure where to start if the beast's wound had been serious.

She huffed. "Is giving a straight answer a foreign concept to you? I know this vagueness isn't a dragon trait."

"Yes, it is." Dragon traditions for careful words and cleverness were well-known among all cultures. In Tiers's case, he still didn't have a solution. Countess Thredsing must be diverted. Perhaps silence would work.

Tiers wrapped a thin bandage around the creature's head, securing it with a spritz of hold spray, and eyed the cat-dragon's injured foot. A foot with barbed scales and sharp claws, possibly sharp enough to pierce his slatesheen-coated skin. "Hold it tightly."

"I have him." Countess Thredsing paused. "And you aren't leaving this house without giving me an answer."

Another yowl escaped the cat-dragon. Tiers allowed his hands to shift to scale form and began treating the cut. "I have no interest in leaving this house unless I am in your company. Your threats are hardly effective."

"Yes, you've mentioned remaining in my company." He looked up to see Countess Thredsing purse her full lips. "And you protected me at the wharf. Protected *me*, specifically, to the exclusion of everyone else."

Alarms rang in his mind, causing his fingers to shake as he began wrapping the bandage around the cut. Would she discover the answer? Part of him hoped she would; her intelligence only increased her allure.

The other part dreaded how she would take the knowledge.

"You can speak in my mind, sometimes. I can hear what you think, sometimes. That can only be one thing, which is … impossible." She focused on him with knife-sharp fierceness. "Isn't it?"

Tiers's heart sank. It seemed they would be having this conversation after all. "You of all people, Countess Thredsing, should know the value of withholding information until the opportune moment."

She glared at him. "Indeed I do, but not when it's withheld from me."

Frustration heated his throat. "I don't know enough! This shouldn't be possible, not unless you have a significant amount of dragon blood. I was going to tell you when I had more information and a cohesive strategy."

"But if you had shared, we could have strategized together. Tell me plainly: are we embermates?"

He nodded. "We appear to have all the signs."

"Yes or no?"

Tiers sighed through clenched teeth. "As much as I can tell, yes."

"Very well." She released the cat-dragon from her grip and walked over to a wall. Her fingers pressed a pattern into a keypad, and a high-pitched screech filled the room. The cat-dragon wrinkled its nose against the sound and yanked its foot away from Tiers. He couldn't blame the beast.

"Damn gadgets," Countess Thredsing muttered.

A second later, a crackly voice echoed through the room. "How can I help you, my lady?"

"I'll be having a guest to dinner tonight. Make the usual preparations. He'll be spending the night as well."

"Shall I ready the guest quarters?"

Countess Thredsing shot Tiers another glare before answering. "Unknown. Since I appear to be his biologically-bound wife, I suppose I should ask him that question."

"His wife? My lady…"

She rolled her eyes. "Ignore that. I misspoke. Set the table and don't worry about a room. That is all."

"Right away, my lady."

Countess Thredsing pressed another series of buttons, and the screech stopped. "I have no idea how dragon mates will hold up in a human court." She turned to Tiers, her hands on her hips. "Do you know?"

He shook his head. "How should I know? This isn't common. In dragon law, we are bound by life and death already, even though our hearts haven't been united. I was going to research human customs on my own."

"Well, now we get to work together." If she let him get a word in edgewise. She continued, "I thought I was fully human with a trace of dragon blood. Tell me how this is physically possible."

He returned her stare, flames burning within him. He spoke

very slowly and clearly, in hopes that she would finally understand and leave him alone to think for a moment. It was difficult enough to endure his own ignorance without having to answer her persistent, annoying questions. "I don't know, Countess. Human-dragon biochemistry isn't my field of study."

"Nor is it mine. But I know that a *strong* dragon bloodline is needed, and I am not aware of any blood of that strength in my family tree." She gritted her teeth. "But considering my parents' history of deception, I shouldn't be surprised. We need answers. Now."

Finally, they were in accord about something.

"Agreed." Tiers walked around the table to join her. The cat-dragon scratched across the table, flapping its wings. "Countess Thredsing, I believe he wants to join us."

She sighed and gave the cat-dragon a distant look that indicated she was using her Talent of sensing value. "Yes, he can come. Somehow, his presence increases our value, which means an increase in our success rate."

"Why?"

Countess Thredsing sighed. "To borrow your favorite phrase, I don't know. Can you carry him?"

"A question. How rare." Tiers picked up the creature and held him close.

Countess Thredsing tsked. "I'll need my hands free to communicate with my contact. She may have information about this secret laboratory the Curious Intrigue uses as a healing center. And she may have insight into our situation." She fixed him with another appraising look. "You may call me Nula. You might as well, considering we're bound together."

At least she was fully acknowledging that.

"Indeed. Call me Tiers."

"Tiers." Her rich voice made the word into an enticing summons that broke through his annoyance. Partly. "Let's go."

He started after her, then paused. Nula's clothing still clung, wet and bedraggled, to her curved figure. "But first, I'd recommend a change of clothing."

Nula paused, then gave a short laugh. "Excellent idea. Perhaps you will have some use after all."

"Such high praise."

She flashed him a smile that fanned the flames inside him higher, and Tiers had to swallow hard. Those very flames would burn her skin if he ever touched her in passion. And given their attraction, keeping his distance would be an increasing burden. The embermate bond was designed to be fulfilled in a surgical heart union and enjoyed in sex. There was no evidence Nula would survive either.

But what would happen when her dragon blood manifested? Would she be able to live with a dual nature without an embermate to anchor her? Would he?

He hoped this contact of Nula's would have answers. Finding the secret laboratory of healing had suddenly become a matter of life and death.

CHAPTER SIX

EMBERMATE. She had a damn embermate.

"How was I supposed to see this coming?" she muttered, glaring at the clothing in her wardrobe as if it had personally offended her. "I'm human!"

Or mostly human. Far too human to have this much blood connection with a dragon, according to what she knew about her family lineage. Another lie her parents had told her. She laughed shortly. "Hardly surprising."

A heavy feeling shadowed her heart, a feeling that persisted no matter how much she buried herself in work or ambition. She was a liar and traitor, the daughter of liars and traitors. The only difference was Nula made it work by lying for the good side and betraying the bad. No one would ever see her differently. Rumors traveled too far and too well for that. But if she had a position and strength, it wouldn't matter what they thought.

Not that it ever had.

She opted for a charcoal gray corset coat and trousers and a crisp white blouse. Sensible flat-soled boots and muted silver earrings completed her ensemble. Before, she had been trying to make a favorable impression on a potential political ally. Now it seemed like she had gotten far more, which was remarkably convenient. The situation called for a business mindset and focus. And her two favorite Starven 500 pistols tucked into secret holsters.

Nula's fingers hovered over her makeup. Maybe just a little. She'd had a difficult day, and it was far from over. She didn't need to look like she'd been put through the depths.

One final look in the mirror. She tweaked everything into place, tied back her braids, and pressed down the silver oval pendant around her neck, her palm lingering above her heart. Dragons endured open-heart surgery with their embermates. But dragons had heartflames, not hearts. Nula didn't know the details, but it stood to reason that these heartflames were more suited to being cut in half than what beat in her chest.

Her fingers closed into a fist. First the fiasco with the dragons at the wharf, and now this. She had dealt with the attack, turning it in her favor. All they had to do was find the dragons and bring them to justice. Now she had to deal with another dragon: Tiers. Admittedly, an attractive dragon. Was that the reason she'd been drawn to him from the start? Was that why his touch made her feel as if something wild and dangerous inside was fighting to be released?

At least he didn't seem intimidated by her. For all his stubbornness, Tiers Sunscaler seemed to welcome her fierceness while still maintaining his own calm independence. It was refreshing. Inviting. Even now, a part of her felt his absence keenly, as if she had always had a space for him.

But what did it mean? She couldn't walk into this situation without knowing anything. There was no guarantee Zilpath would have any information. And knowing Zilpath, even if she had information, she might not share it.

Nula groaned and turned away from her mirror, rubbing her

forehead. Her eyes fell upon another mirror across her bedroom: her private clipse-mirror, suspended between two twisted brass holders.

She had access to one source of information. That source might not know any more than she did but might be willing to help figure things out.

Nula strode across the room, her boots loud on the tiled floor. She pressed her fingers to the mirror's ridged surface. After a quick code entry, Kesia Ironfire stared back at her. The dragon woman's brown hair was pulled up tightly in the stern buns preferred in the Scepter of Knowledge, but her expression was open and curious.

"Nula? What's happening?" She paused. "I mean, how are you? That's the correct human phrase, right?"

Nula nodded shortly. "I told you, those greetings don't matter to me. I need your help with a concern regarding Tiers Sunscaler."

Kesia's amber eyes stared to the side for a moment, a sign that she was communicating with her embermate, Zephryn. "Interesting. Zephryn says that Tiers has contacted him as well. They are speaking at this moment. Something must have really gone wrong on your mission."

So that's why the stupid dragon wanted to use the spare office. Nula should have guessed. Though why wouldn't he just tell her?

"Are all dragons terrible at communication, or is Tiers just defective?"

Kesia raised her eyebrows. "I don't think he's defective. You've read his dossier."

"Which simply says he's a diplomat and an administrator." Nula flopped into a chair near the clipse-mirror.

The dragon woman paused for a moment. Her eyes drifted to the side again, and her head tilted. Then her brow furrowed, and she turned her focus back to Nula. "Given what has transpired between Sunscaler and you, I suppose I can tell you. He's the administrator of dragon espionage activity. He has been for years. We're very satisfied with his cautiousness, since that's part of his office, but as his embermate, it must be frustrating."

Nula leaned forward, grateful for Kesia and Zephryn's mental link. It saved her a lot of conversation. "Yes, the embermate business. What does that mean for a human?"

"How would I know? It isn't common, and I'm not a caregiver."

"Granted." Nula rubbed her forehead again. She would have to reapply the powder there later. "What about between dragons?"

Kesia frowned. "That was over ten years ago. I was a child. Zephryn and I connected before we met. Our heart-need had unparalleled strength."

Nula jumped on the word. "Heart-need? What does that mean? It can't be romantic longing."

"Well … no. That became part of it when we got older, even though we weren't aware of it." The dragon's pale skin flushed pink. "The heart-need is more of a biological instinct. Once embermates are revealed to each other, their heartflames become incomplete when separate. They must be joined together or else."

"Or else what?"

Kesia's eyes turned to slits, a sign of distress. "Zephryn says the result would be death. Which was why Lord Garishton needed to allow me to bond with Zephryn. Not doing so would have killed both of us." She snorted out a greenish plume of smoke. "And his precious experiment would have died as well."

Yes. The mysterious green smoke, able to nullify Talents, that was overtaking Kesia's body. Nula placed her hand over her chest again. "But you're both dragons. I'm human. Surely that wouldn't—"

"I don't know, Nula." Dark red scales tinged with green peppered Kesia's forehead and cheekbones, another sign that she was upset. "But Tiers is a full-blooded dragon. Separation from you would kill him."

"No." The word came out as a growl. Nula glared at the clipse-mirror. "That is unacceptable."

"I understand. And I agree with Zephryn. You need to find answers as soon as possible. This is just as important as finding those two dragons."

"I know!" Nula shouted, slapping her hands on the desk. She stood, anger and frustration heating her veins and burning her eyes.

"Nula! Your—"

"What?"

"Your eyes. For a moment, they flashed with dragon fire."

Nula squinted and rubbed her eyelids, trying to control her irritation. This couldn't be happening. She didn't need to turn into a dragon or a half-dragon or whatever else was eating away at her.

But it was happening. There was no point in pretending otherwise.

Nula squared her shoulders and pushed down the fear. She could handle this. "Maybe this is fortuitous."

Kesia tilted her head. "How so?"

"Two dragons. Myself and Tiers. A far more even playing field."

"I don't think it works like that—"

Nula palmed off the screen. There was no time to waste. She reached the spare office in a matter of seconds and threw open the door. It was caught almost immediately. Her heart skipped when she saw Tiers on the other side. His lips pulled into a smirk that didn't quite touch the gravity and relief in his eyes.

"I see you understand the value of additional insight as well," he said with an off-kilter cadence hinting at humor.

Nula sighed, her shoulders relaxing despite her frustration. The prickling sensations beneath her skin increased. "Was Zephryn any help?"

"Only as much as he could be, given that he isn't a caregiver or a scientist."

"Kesia was the same. Apparently if we don't figure out this embermate business, you could die."

"You could as well."

She didn't know what startled her more, the thought that she could die or the fact that Tiers sounded truly concerned. Yet it was clear on his face, as it always had been. Honest compassion and caring.

Her heart warmed. But she couldn't trust it. A bond was one matter. Feelings were another matter entirely.

"Oh? Kesia didn't mention that."

"Zephryn was only making logical inferences. He didn't have any proof. We need to do further research. Is this clothing suitable?"

Nula sighed. Couldn't he dress himself? Well, he was a newcomer to human society, and the clothing had been selected from spare Lawless reserves. She cleared her throat and began pacing in front of him, eyeing him critically. "The black pants fit well enough, especially around the hips. The cream shirt is a little loose, but the cut of the vest takes care of that. And, well, the collar is meant to be tied with a cravat, not open to show skin, but the Scepter of Commerce isn't as formal as the other Scepters…"

Nula's voice trailed off as she gave him a final once-over, forcing herself to look at his face. His warm, tawny skin drew her in, as did the smirk playing at his lips and the glint in his eyes that indicated he was all too aware of her approval.

She put her hands on her hips. "Did you do that on purpose?"

"Did you honestly think I would travel to a human city without being aware of the local attire?" Tiers raked a hand through his black hair. "Really, Nula. You aren't the only prepared person in the room."

Her mouth dropped open. "You were the one who asked! And considering how inept Ironfire and Nightstalker were on their first trip here—"

"As former political prisoners, their graces are to be judged by entirely different standards." Tiers slipped past her smoothly. "We don't have time to waste. If you could direct us?"

She rolled her eyes. "Yes. This way."

"What of our furry friend?"

Nula glanced down to see the cat-dragon staring up at her intently. "You want to come along?"

The cat-dragon sniffed, then hobbled past them into the depths of the mansion.

Tiers chuckled. "I guess that's your answer."

Hopefully the odd beast wouldn't break anything.

She turned back to the situation with her embermate. Nula didn't know what was more shocking—that the dragon had managed to wrest control of the conversation from her, or that she didn't want to kill him for it. Seeing as how they were both trying to avoid their deaths, killing Tiers would be counterproductive.

For now.

It wasn't until they were in a groundcar and nearly at Zilpath's shop that Nula realized Tiers had managed to divert her attention away from his conversation with Zephryn. She didn't expect him to share all the details, but that didn't mean she wouldn't fight for them anyway. There was something deceptively relaxing about Tiers's independent nature that made it easy to fall into silence and deal with her own matters, trusting that he would be an equal partner in whatever they faced.

She couldn't lapse into such a dangerous habit. As soon as they spoke with Zilpath, Nula would confront him again.

They entered the narrow shop with its layers of bright fabrics and garments on every flat surface and hanging from the ceiling. Nula breathed in the richly perfumed air and exhaled slowly. Safety. Just like it was when she'd first come here, over fifteen years ago.

The sound of a pistol cocking broke her reverie.

Tiers's breath caught. "Nula—"

She turned to see Zilpath standing there, pistol in hand, her green eyes sharp.

Nula shook her head, fighting to keep a smile off her face. The dragon deserved a little fear for his stunt with the clothing. "It's all right, Tiers. I suppose I deserve it. Do your worst, Zilpath, old friend."

Chapter Seven

NULA WAS IN DANGER. Everything within Tiers clamored for him to obliterate the old woman holding the Berringer pistol. The only thing staying his hand was the small voice in his mind reminding him that Zilpath Irudha was staunchly on the side of the Lawless.

The old woman's index finger drifted toward the trigger, her unwavering gaze on Nula. Tiers's mind spun. This had to be a mistake. The records stated that Zilpath had proven her loyalty many times over, despite her attitude.

His heartflame confirmed this. And it was almost never wrong.

Nula's gray eyes gleamed and narrowed, then she threw back her head and laughed. It was a bell-like sound, filling the room with warmth and ease. Zilpath lowered the weapon,

and an answering grin spread across her face. Her shoulders shook with mirth as she set the gun down, walked around the counter with a little hop-skip, and embraced Nula, who hugged her close.

Only then did Tiers register what Nula had said. *Old friend.* The women knew each other.

Nula had tricked him.

He huffed out a stream of smoke and leaned back against a shelf. Nula and Zilpath stepped away from each other, and his embermate shot him a knowing glance. He returned her stare.

"You continue to surprise me with fresh secrets, Nula."

"A trait we share, yes?"

Her mouth smiled, but her eyes turned as grave as stones. Tiers's throat tightened. She knew he hadn't told her everything. Well, she would just have to wait for information about Yaron and Jylle. Especially regarding his friendship with Yaron.

Guilt weighted his stomach, but he pushed it aside. Some things didn't need to be shared. They were embermates; they would have a long time to share personal issues. The fact that Yaron was a threat was all Nula needed to know.

A smacking sound diverted Tiers's attention back to Zilpath. Her fingers were flying through a series of complicated swipes and gestures, far too fast for him to catch every word. He'd only learned a handful of phrases in pidsyn before coming to the Scepter of Commerce. A pity, since everyone in the city and surrounding countryside seemed to know the business sign language. Children were taught it in school. An incredibly useful tool, since Zilpath's tongue had been cut out during her enslavement. In the Scepter of Commerce, she was able to conduct all activities as normal.

For her part, Nula was engaging in a lively conversation, her fingers moving with fluid elegance. He coughed. "Would you care to translate?"

"Oh, you want information?" Nula pursed her lips in mock surprise. Zilpath tugged on Nula's braids with a look of remonstrance worthy of Tiers's mother. Nula sighed. "Very well. She says she's tried to track down the Curious Intrigue's healing facility before, but the agents she sent out disappeared."

"That's discouraging." But not surprising. Until the recent breakthrough with the crown prince and his princess, there was little reason to investigate one suspicious facility. Securing Nightstalker and Ironfire and maintaining the stronghold at Edgefell Peaks had been a far greater priority. "So she doesn't have any active intel?"

Zilpath's fingers began moving rapidly again. Nula translated, "With the recent takedown of facilities, it's easier to track the outliers still operating outside the Lawless, the Scepter of Commerce council, or major organized crime. There are five possible locations."

Five. Wonderful. His expression must have showed his irritation because Zilpath shot him a sour look and made a few additional gestures. Tiers looked to Nula to translate, but she only chuckled. Her expression fell serious as Zilpath continued. She tsked, but translated, "She says my parents could possibly help narrow down the search." Nula glared at Zilpath. "Even though I've told her they don't have any relevant information. They've been interrogated multiple times."

"By you?"

It was a deliberately cruel question. Tiers knew enough about human culture to understand the politeness codes, but he couldn't help himself. If Nula continued to needle him about his secrets, he would give her the same treatment. She had her own secrets, and they needed to come out.

Nula turned her glare on him, then tsked again. "No, though considering their lies about my bloodline, perhaps the time has come for me to ask the questions. As my embermate, I'm sure you'll be willing to assist?"

Tiers only lifted his chin. "As you have need."

"Good."

Zilpath yanked her arm, her fingers spiraling through fresh questions. Nula grimaced and looked at Tiers. "I'm going to tell her about our embermate situation."

The shopkeeper's eyes widened as Nula gestured her way through the explanation, and she sat down abruptly, plucking at her baggy flowered dress. Once Nula's fingers stopped, Zilpath clasped her hand and squeezed it. Nula's face softened. For the first time, Tiers saw fear and anxiety written across her features, along with something warmer, something open.

The last expression tore at him. She wanted to trust someone, even if she didn't realize it. It was a desire he understood all too well. His own heartflame leaped in response, pounding hard against his chest, yearning to be connected with her, to share her pain and joy, to be bound to her so they breathed as one.

Nula met his gaze, and he swallowed. For a moment, fire flashed behind her eyes and nothing else seemed important. Then her expression wrenched. She pressed her lips together and fell against the counter with a hiss of pain. Zilpath grabbed her and waved him over. She pointed to the back of Nula's hands. They seemed to be bulging with ripples.

Tiers traced a finger over her skin before he could stop himself. In response, Nula's shoulders slumped, and her eyes closed. The stirrings under her skin slowed and disappeared.

"Well. Maybe I need to get more sleep." She gave a short laugh, opened her eyes, and stood, tugging at her corset-coat and tossing her braids over her shoulder.

His heart sank. "You know that isn't what happened."

"Then what did?" she snapped.

Tiers met her gaze. "I don't know. But it may have something to do with your dragon blood, and the need to seal the heartflame bond." He looked at Zilpath. "Do you know anything?"

Her fingers began signing.

Nula blinked and shook her head, her usual arrogant mask falling into place. "She says she knows some in the resistance who come from dragon and human blood. The pairings are rare. She isn't aware of any that are within the vicinity of this city."

"Yes, Zephryn said the same thing." Tiers reached out and stroked the back of her hand again.

She relaxed, then tensed, almost an afterthought. "What else did he say? You need to talk. Both of you." A faint smile curved her lips. "Just not at the same time."

Words spilled from him freely. "Zephryn recalled that before he and Kesia were bound when they were young, they spent all their time in each other's company. The same is true for other dragons I know. Separation from an embermate before bonding causes physical pain."

"Which is why you refused to leave my side earlier."

"Yes."

Zilpath's fingers moved. Nula watched her intently, then nodded. "She says the few mixed-bloods she's met have manifestations of their dragon heritage in some way. This could possibly be part of that, though it should have manifested in me earlier. My parents may have had something to do with repressing it. She says I shouldn't fight it, and that your presence should assist with the transformation, since we are embermates, and … now she's going into a religious discussion about destiny never being wrong."

Tiers remembered that Nula could sense value and extrapolate that value into future possibilities. "Do you agree?"

"Perhaps. Yes. I mean—" She paused, her eyes distant as she

used her Talent. Sweat beaded on her forehead, then she sagged down on the counter again, her eyes rolling back in her head.

Tiers caught her, one arm beneath her knees and the other supporting her back. His heart hammered in his chest. Was she all right? Anger and concern flared within him. Despite his emotions, his mind was crystal clear. She needed to get home.

Zilpath began swiping in the air. He shook his head. "You know I won't understand that."

She made an impatient gesture, then pulled out a pad of paper and a pen, scribbling down a note. She held out the paper to him. **Take care of her. She's all I have in Sekastra. She dies, you die.**

"Yes, that's true."

Zilpath glared at him and scribbled down more words. **I will find a way to kill you twice.**

Well, that was comforting. "Noted."

Tiers started walking toward the door, but Zilpath smacked her pad on the counter, drawing his attention to her once more. "What is it this time?"

One tablespoon Qorus liquor dissolved in warm milk with a dash of norimund. Have that ready as soon as she wakes. I'll come by as soon as I can. Bonilus give you peace.

"Thank you." Tiers nodded and left the shop. He was keenly aware of the woman in his arms, her every breath reliant on him and some mysterious transformation that so few people knew about. His chest tightened as he got into the groundcar. Somehow, he managed a suitable excuse for the driver.

He held her close, tracing the edge of her cheekbone.

All-Maker, keep her. Religion had never interested him beyond the odd philosophical musing, but at that moment, Tiers would welcome any peace he could get.

An engine was perched on her chest.

Nula tried to push it aside, but it seemed to grow heavier. A rough-softness brushed against her cheek, and a chuckle came from somewhere to her left.

Where *was* she?

"Freckles, you need to move so she can breathe freely."

A rusty meow came from the object on her chest. Nula opened her eyes and stared into the face of the cat-dragon. Its green eyes observed her calmly, then it licked her cheek a few times and moved over to the other side of her bed.

Confusion flicked through her mind. She was in her bed. In her room, with the tapestries on the walls, the chifforobe in the corner, and little else. Why was she here? She should be in Zilpath's shop trying to get answers about the secret Curious Intrigue facility and the embermate dilemma.

"What happened?"

"You passed out in the shop. I brought you here to rest." Tiers Sunscaler. Nula turned to where he sat next to her bed, holding a mug of something that smelled of childhood. His expression was calm, but worry tightened his eyes.

"Did Zilpath tell you to make that?"

"Yes. She was quite adamant that you should drink it."

"Huh. Of course she was." Nula pressed her palms into the bed, raising herself to a seated position, and reached for the mug. "It's one of her favorite remedies." She breathed the savory scent of norimund and the nutty tang of Qorus liquor, then took a sip. A fragile calm filled her as the familiar beverage made its way into her stomach. "I met Zilpath when I was twelve, shortly after I had learned that my parents were terrible people. She made this for me to help me cope. She said that if it helped her after she escaped her slave owner, it could help me feel less enslaved to my parents."

"Your parents owned you?"

"After a fashion." Nula paused. There was little point in hiding it from him. She took another sip of her drink. This time, it settled uneasily in her stomach. "They'd never admit it, but they treated me like their finest acquisition. You'll see what I mean when you meet them. I'll contact Zilpath to set that up." She sighed. "What a wasted trip."

She moved to get up. Tiers held out a hand in protest as Nula's muscles gave out. He caught the mug before it fell. She sagged back onto her pillows, feeling helpless. Useless.

"*I'll* contact her later. You need to rest."

"You think she'll talk with *you* to set up the meeting?"

He raised his eyebrows. "Contrary to certain opinions, I actually am a capable dragon."

"I know. But…" Nula fisted her hand and pounded it against the blanket "I'm sorry. I'm not used to this … feeling. This strange connection that leaves me vulnerable."

"You're not alone in that." Tiers paused, his elegant face stern with thought. He gave a deep sigh. "One of the dragons who attacked us this morning was my fleetwing. Unbonded dragons are paired up as tactical partners. We had been friends since childhood."

A shadow passed over his face, along with an expression Nula knew all too well. She had seen it enough in the mirror. Regret mixed with a rock-hard determination to do what was necessary, no matter the cost.

"What happened?"

"My parents were founding members of the Lawless. I was ten at the time. They gave me the choice to stay with them as double agents or go into hiding." He paused. "I had to help, and I wanted Yaron to understand. I thought he would understand." Pain flashed in his eyes. "Even now, I have no regrets."

His eyes met hers, fathomless with intensity. An intensity her own heart leaped to match.

"Because you had to do something. You couldn't stand by and let others get away with doing what was wrong."

Tiers nodded and set the mug on a nearby table. "I knew I could do it and do it well. And I have. Alone."

"It's the only way, right?" Her voice was soft. "Even if everyone hates you or distrusts you, you get the job done. You *win*. And when everything is over, you get what's yours."

"Ours." Tiers gave a crooked smile. "We are embermates. We are in this together now." He paused. "And is getting what's yours really the only reason you fight?"

Nula stared at her hands. Part of her wanted to trust him, to tell him everything, then pull him into bed next to her and find rest. But it had been less than a day since this began. And the last time he had touched her hand, she'd felt like exploding from the heat and pressure of *becoming*. Becoming what, Nula had no idea, and neither did anyone else. That was reason enough to keep up her distance, even if Tiers's presence calmed her.

There were still many things he didn't need to know right now.

"We should move on to more important matters." She cleared her throat and pulled what was left of her dignity around her. "For instance, sharing relevant intel on dragons in the Scepter of Commerce and discussing what skills we have in order to work together more effectively." She set her teeth and shifted until she was sitting up again with her feet resting on the ground. Her muscles seemed to be holding this time. The cat-dragon gave a curious mreow, hobbling into place beside her.

"Very well." Tiers offered her his arm, his expression shifting to neutral.

Nula was tempted to ignore him but thought it might be better to take a little assistance now rather than embarrass herself later. She scratched the cat-dragon's head, then grabbed Tiers's arm and pulled herself off the bed. "What did you call that beast?"

"What, Freckles?" He smiled. <He needed a name. Considering the golden scales on his coat, I thought it fitting.>

Somehow, the mindspeak didn't shock her anymore. It felt as natural as speaking aloud.

There was no need to read into it. Embermates had that sort of bond.

<Indeed. I like it.> She scooped up the cat-dragon with her free arm. His wings fluttered, and he settled in her arms with a warm, satisfying weight. There was a slightly accusing, judgmental look in his eyes, though, as if he knew she had held back from Tiers.

What did Freckles know, anyway? She was making wise decisions. There was no need to make this association with Tiers Sunscaler too personal.

A memory flashed through her mind. Dayevid, grinning at her across the table with a winsome glint in his blue eyes. Dayevid, collapsed on the ground with several bullet wounds in his chest. Her heart tightened, and she gritted her teeth.

Never mind what Tiers said or how he treated her. Things getting personal never ended well.

CHAPTER EIGHT

YARON SUMMONED HIM THAT NIGHT.

<Wake up, Tiers. You sleep too much.>

Tiers jolted awake, his breath shallow, dragon claws emerging from his fingertips and digging into the side of the bed.

<You never had any boundaries, Yaron.>

<You always had too many.>

Sweat beaded Tiers's brow, and he shoved down his fear. Mental contact should be impossible. Unbonded dragons could mindspeak only when in sight of each other. However, in the case of fleetwings who were not embermates, there was an additional transferal of blood to enable a strong connection, as if with siblings. At times, Tiers and Yaron had been able to bridge the mental divide and speak from a distance, similar to the strong ties of dragon twins.

It appeared even a long absence was insufficient to break their bond entirely.

<It's not too late for you to see reason.> Yaron's voice held the same diffident, reckless tone it always had, but this time it was undergirded with concern. <Why protect the human?>

<We chose our sides long ago.> Tiers sat up in his bed in a corner of Nula's bedchambers. She'd requested the separation, since

they had only just met. He yearned to be in the same bed as her, but he could lock that desire away along with all the other things he'd denied himself throughout his life.

Including his closest friendship.

Yaron chuckled. <What happened? You feel as if you've eaten a sick mountain grazer.>

Despite himself, Tiers sighed wistfully. <Nothing so good as that in the city.>

By human standards, Nula's food had been quite acceptable. By dragon standards, it lacked the satisfaction of raw meat hunted from the air. At the very least, next time he should request his meat portion far rarer. As for the mealtime conversation, it had focused on their individual qualifications as espionage leaders, with both revealing knowledge strategically. The only thing that kept it from being a mutual interrogation was the lack of intimidating environments, the free exchange of ideas, and Nula's own intoxicating presence.

The woman had no idea how irresistible she was when flustered by his comebacks to her forceful declarations.

<Who are you thinking about, Tiers?>

Fewmets. He shunted his emotions aside. <None of your concern. Get out of my mind.>

<You can't have feelings for her.>

Tiers glared into the dim air. <I said the same to you when you were bound to a zealous dragon who torched human settlements for pleasure.>

<All humans are enemies. She showed me that. Good thing, too. I had nearly swallowed your traitorous lies.>

Tiers stood and walked over to the wall. Nula's bedroom lacked windows for better structural integrity, but he could sense the open air on the other side, beckoning him to fly. However, in a city as crowded and anxious as the Scepter of Commerce, that was the opposite of wisdom. <I assume your flame-eager embermate is taking as many lives as she can while you recuperate? I've heard the Low Quarter has an abundance of humans considered worthless.>

<Yes, but it is difficult for her to do as much as she'd like, with these troublesome law enforcement officers. And as my fleetwing, her presence aids my own healing.>

Tiers traced a pattern in a wall tapestry, admiring the fine work. The weaver was nearly as skilled as his parents had been before the war, back when they had been textile creators, weaving garments from metal and gemstone threads. It was something Tiers himself had a skill for. Not that it mattered, except as a personal hobby.

<Trying to ignore me?>

Tiers kept his tone level. <Don't you ever shut up?>

<Speaking makes this room seem less stifling. Annoying you is a bonus. At least your prison is closer to the sky.>

He was underground, then. Perhaps in the city's sewer network? It was a start, in any case. The fact that Yaron knew Tiers's location was surprising enough. But it wouldn't be difficult to learn that Tiers was housed in Nula's cave through the rumors of servants. In any case, Nula's mansion was well-fortified. She'd told him at supper that she preferred her enemies to believe they had her pinned. It made surprising them easier.

Skies above, he could see how their hearts had aligned. If only they could overcome the rest.

<You are bound to the human, aren't you? Your feelings betray you.>

Tiers blew out a stream of smoke. <Only interested in her as a meal, I assure you.>

<A weak jest, coming from you. You are entranced. Very interesting.>

<Return to your pit, Yaron. We will find you soon.>

<If you're still alive.>

Yaron's presence left his mind. Tiers gritted his teeth and pounded his fist into the wall, causing a few stones to bend outward.

"A nightmare?"

Nula. He turned to see her keen gray eyes observing him in the darkness. Could she actually see him? Was that enhancement part of her transformation? He turned his mind back to her question. "Something like that, I suppose."

For once, he was grateful for the absence of their bond. It made lying far easier. And for the present, he needed that advantage. Just for a little longer, until he could deal with Yaron. She would understand once it was all over.

"So it wasn't a nightmare." Nula's tone was flat, and she shook her head, tugging at the silk scarf that bound her hair away from her face. Her eyes softened. "I was wrong. Separation was a foolish idea. We're already married in dragon culture, and that is enough for me. This bed is very large. You could easily sleep on the other side."

Yes. He could.

Next to her, the cat-dragon gave a soft mewl, studying Tiers expectantly, almost accusingly. Strange. Neither of them knew how aware the creature was. Could he actually be cognizant of what was happening between him and Nula? No. The late night must be playing tricks on his mind.

"Well, as you will." Nula tsked. Tiers gave her a second glance, noticing the shadows under her eyes. She still bore symptoms from what had happened earlier that day. No matter what secrets separated them, her life was irrevocably bound to his. Unto death, it seemed.

After a moment, he walked to the other side of her bed and got beneath the covers, making sure to keep space between them. The mattress was firmer than he expected, with a layer of cushion that made it comfortable without being excessive.

Not that it mattered. After his conversation with Yaron, Tiers didn't anticipate sleeping at all.

He needed to plan.

Chapter Nine

HER EMBERMATE WAS ANXIOUS. It radiated from Tiers as he and Nula stood, waiting for the groundcar to arrive.

He had been uneasy for two days as they waited for clearances to see her parents. The Grand Count Nul and his wife, Grand Countess Hrelana, were highly-guarded war prisoners, particularly because of their Talents. Nula should have known better than to expect a quick audience, even if she was their daughter.

Especially because she was their daughter.

The delay had left her and Tiers with time to conduct their own research and business. Tiers had made himself at home in her spare office. Considering their predicament of needing to be in each other's company nearly every moment, she had opted to stay in his office instead of using hers.

They were breaking down barriers at an alarmingly easy rate, judging by their bed situation. Never mind that they fell asleep separated, each on their own side. Both mornings had found them closer together, although not quite touching, while a smug-looking Freckles sprawled across the bottom of the bed.

It was a novelty, sleeping with someone without any other activities taking place. Sensing the presence of the other, their quiet inhale and exhale. Trusting that they wouldn't kill you in your sleep. Logically, Tiers couldn't, since it would harm him as well.

It was oddly reassuring and … nice.

Not that he needed to be told that.

She was starting to wonder if keeping silent about her feelings meant anything. Given how Tiers's concern filtered through their joined hands, Nula guessed he could sense the spinning of her thoughts, especially the dread she felt about seeing her parents. As long as he didn't ask about the dread, then all would be well.

Right now, she didn't need the distraction of personal conversation, especially about emotions.

Freckles hovered next to them, head held high and green eyes bright and curious. The cat-dragon had apparently declared himself well enough to travel.

Considering where they were going, Nula didn't have the heart to make him stay behind. Besides, she could use every ally at her disposal.

Nula squeezed Tiers's hand. <Worrying won't protect us from an attack.>

Tiers stared down at her as the groundcar pulled up beside the curb. <You never know. It could be my hidden Talent. Anxiety-induced marvels. Or perhaps attacking others with my mind.>

<That would be far more useful.> She dropped his hand as they entered the vehicle. Freckles curled up on the middle part of the seat between them, apparently having overcome his fear of groundcars. "I've never understood why some dragons are Talentless. It never happens among humans."

His eyes slitted in thought. "It is peculiar. It started happening in my parents' generation and became more prevalent in mine. Before that, there are no records of Talentless dragons."

"Do you think the Curious Intrigue had something to do with it?"

"That's one theory, especially considering how Princess Ironfire was experimented on with the Talent-cancelling green smoke. But removing Talents from dragons loyal to the Pinnacle doesn't make any sense. Talented dragons are more powerful warriors for the Curious Intrigue. Why would they deny themselves an advantage?"

Nula shrugged. "But since the war is staged, that wouldn't matter. And dragons with Talents would be harder to control."

"True. But the Pinnacle has other ways of controlling us. There must be another reason."

He drifted off in thought, his fingers tapping at the side of the car. Nula tsked. He had a habit of doing that, and it still annoyed her. Yet it tended to produce more useful results than if she pushed with questions right away, so she held off and petted the cat-dragon instead.

A few moments later, the car stopped outside a low, one-story building in the High Quarter. It was inlaid with glimmering mosaics in a rainbow of colors and intricate panes of window-glass.

Tiers raised his eyebrows. "A jewelry store?"

"Don't worry, Tiers. You're exempt from having to buy me anything. Wedding jewelry faded as a custom in the Scepter of Commerce years ago. Only the Scepter of Pleasure indulges in it."

"I see. So we are here, then?"

"Indeed. The pretense is to sell some jewelry in exchange for dels, for money. It's the best present a woman could give herself, yes?"

"And I thought only dragons created hoards."

Nula flashed him a smile that he returned with a glint in his golden eyes. They exited the groundcar, waited for Freckles to fly out and land in Tiers's arms, then walked to the entrance, an arched doorway inlaid with bronze filigree. Inside were no fewer than ten guards in immaculate suits, stationed around glass display cases filled with sparkling jewelry draped atop velvet-cover stands.

She studied the saleswoman, a matronly woman with a coif of gray hair and a well-tailored black dress. "Pardon me?"

The woman looked up. "Can I help you, my lady?"

"Yes. I need to sell some very valuable necklaces."

The saleswoman nodded and pulled out a length of black velvet, which she draped over the counter. "Certainly. Please lay them here for preliminary appraisal."

Nula tsked. "I'm afraid I can't risk such exposure. Do you have a private viewing area?"

"I'm sorry to say we do not, my lady." The saleswoman's expression didn't change. Nula focused on her with her Talent for a moment, then relaxed. From her tightly bound hair to her firm smile, the woman radiated constancy and purpose. Highly valuable, and ideal for her role as keeper of a secret prison.

Time to show the password.

"A pity. We were hoping to purchase a ring." And then a significant glance at a particular painting of a seal on the wall.

Then, because she was looking around anyway, Nula glanced at Tiers. He had returned to a stoic posture. It didn't quite hide the fact that he was a deadly dragon, ready to follow her lead but not like a senseless lackey. He'd proven his independence many times, and even managed to deal with her when she was unconscious. Perhaps she had found a worthy partner.

Heat rose in Nula's throat. To top it all off, he was handsome. And he was holding Freckles as if he actually cared about the cat-dragon.

She turned back to the saleswoman, whose brown eyes had narrowed slightly. "Well, I'm afraid my husband and I will have to go elsewhere."

"It appears you must." The saleswoman made a small gesture with her right hand. "Apologies, my lady. Please take the exit in the back. It is far more pleasant."

Pleasant. That was it. The code for entrance, according to Nula's contact. "Thank you."

Nula walked toward the back entrance and silently waited as Tiers made his way across the room. He tilted his head. "Husband, hmm? Was that part of the official code word exchange?"

She smirked. "Yes, because I said so. Although there can be a variety of pairings. But you're my embermate, so you're stuck with me."

"A situation I am all too happy to endure."

Freckles flicked his scaly tail at Nula with a soft mreow as the floor beneath them lowered with a creak of machinery and a whirring of gears. Tiers grabbed her hand protectively.

<Don't worry. This is supposed to happen.> Nula squeezed his hand, feeling the odd pressure beneath her skin again, as if something was trying to emerge. With Tiers nearby, the sensation came more frequently, but his constant presence helped to ease the pain it brought.

Around them were smooth walls embedded with faint lights. The secret elevator descended for several minutes, finally stopping deep under the earth. Before them, a door slid open, revealing a small hallway of dark metal with the same faint recessed lights set into squares along the wall. A thick steel door loomed at the end.

They strode toward the door. Upon closer inspection, it revealed a code-circle dial with various letters, numbers, and symbols to be spun into the right locations. Nula trailed her fingers over the correct combination, turning the dials one way, then another, to lock into the mechanism. The door swung open.

She almost wished it hadn't. Then she could pretend none of this existed. She cleared her throat. "Let me do the talking, all right? They're dangerous people."

"As always, I will act with discretion and good judgment."

She turned to face Tiers. "I'm serious about this. Not a word."

He stared down at her calmly. "And I'm serious about ensuring that we get the information we need. It is very likely that will involve my silence, but if it doesn't," he took her hand, <I will endeavor to let you hear my words first.>

<It's a deal. Let's move along, shall we?>

She dropped his hand and continued down through the prison. His stubbornness made sense. After all, they'd just met each other, and she had just been admiring his independence. Nula couldn't expect him to trust her implicitly. They were allies on a mission to find the rogue dragons and ensure the safe ascension of the civil council. The last two days had built an oddly solid foundation between them, borne out of the embermate bond.

This meeting would test that bond.

They walked down a hallway of gray steel walls. Periodically, a square door broke up the monotony. The only sound was their shoes on the floor.

"Isolation cells," Nula said, her voice flat. "Each one observed every hour, day and night, with clipse-mirrors and spy-commers embedded in the walls. For the most difficult prisoners." She paused. "My parents aren't here."

He raised his eyebrows. "Then where are they?"

"They negotiated certain conditions with the Lawless when

they were taken into custody."

The hallway ended abruptly—or so it appeared. Nula pulled out a pair of goggles from her purse and put them on, pressing a few buttons along the side. Special lenses snapped over her field of vision, washing the room around her in varying shades of red. She glanced at Tiers.

He flared dark red, the color radiating from his chest and outlining his entire body. His heartflame. Nula reached out and pressed her palm against his warmth, breathing slowly and smoothly, tasting smoke and ash. Another scent assailed her, one that she had never noticed before: the smooth flavor of pepricorns, known for their subtle hints and sharp, biting finish. She licked her lips, swallowing the flavor. The familiar pressure built beneath her skin, fighting to surface. Her heart sped up, and her fingers slowly moved across his chest.

Tiers cleared his throat, releasing a soft wisp of smoke as he stepped toward her. <Nula, what are you doing?>

She paused. <Your smell…>

<Ah, yes. Dragon embermates have distinct scents to each other. It appears that ours have surfaced. You smell of wheatsimmer, a golden liquor of dragons.> He shifted the cat-dragon in his arms and placed his hand over hers, the contact slowing the rippling pressure under her skin, though not lessening its intensity. Freckles turned in his arms, his slitted green eyes drifting between Nula and the dragon as if watching some fascinating game.

It certainly was to Nula. Tiers was most fascinating, more than any man she'd seen or been with. She should say something, instead of standing there like an idiot.

"Your heartflame … it calls to me."

"As does yours to me," he said. "But we don't know what it

means. Not fully. We must be cautious."

His words were cold water to the heat. Even an embermate, a biologically-destined spouse, couldn't be relied on. As usual, she could only rely on herself. She set her jaw. "Well, that is very inconvenient." She sighed. "My apologies. I'm sure I'm only trying to distract myself from what comes next."

She tried to pull her hand away, but Tiers held it fast, pulsing warmth into her skin. "You have no need to apologize, Nula."

The way he said her name, softly but firmly with dragon resonance, was undergirded with desire that was all the more tempting because he didn't give in to it. The potent need lay there, just beneath his fathomless eyes and calm, elegant features. It heated her palm through his chest—a chest muscled like the warrior he could be when he chose. A powerful man with no need to claim the spotlight.

Damn, this dragon would be the end of her.

Freckles gave another rough, crackly meow, breaking through her thoughts. His green eyes bored into hers as if challenging her distaste for the upcoming conversation. Had the cat-dragon been given some kind of intelligence-boosting serum while in the laboratory? Or was he just being annoying? He seemed to have an infernal sense of her thoughts and feelings.

It didn't matter. It was time to face what was on the other side of the wall.

Nula pulled her hand away from Tiers's hold and turned around. Thanks to her goggles, the outline of a doorway was clearly visible in pale red lines against the blank wall. Next to the door was a smaller square, indicating a reflective palm reader. She placed her hand on it, and the door slid into the wall.

"Remember, let me do the talking. You can't trust either of them."

Tiers nodded. "Any particular reason why?"

Nerves and pent-up tension released her tongue. "Since you insist on knowing," she said, flashing him a mirthless grin, "they're responsible for killing the last man I fell in love with."

She stalked through the door before he could ask any more questions.

Time for one hell of a family reunion.

Chapter Ten

NULA'S WORDS ECHOED through his mind as he followed her into the room. Her parents had the man killed? There had been no indication of any serious affairs in Nula's dossier

He sighed. Of course there weren't. Nula was a spy, same as him. If she had fallen in love, such vulnerability would have been a severe liability in the field. She would have had to handle it with extreme discretion, if she dared explore the feelings at all.

That presumed that what she'd told him was true and not a diversion meant to send his mind spinning in circles. But that wasn't like her. Nula was many things—a relentlessly stubborn woman among them—but she prized honesty above all else. She cleverly used that bluntness whenever anyone challenged her, layering it with half-truths and intimidation when necessary.

A remarkable woman.

"Careful, Sir Dragon. Your throat is heating up. And, dare I say, other regions as well?"

The voice was light and silky, pitched with perfect clarity. He glanced around, repressing his irritation at Nula for steering his thoughts off track. A liability indeed. They needed to seal this bond soon so he could continue his diplomatic and espionage duties properly.

They stood in a small entryway. In front of them, a thick panel of clear glass formed the fourth wall of two cells. Each cell held one prisoner so visitors could see both at once, but the prisoners couldn't see each other.

Nula tsked in annoyance, her hands on her hips. "Well, Mother, you and Father would be the ones to know about following uncontrollable physical urges."

"Oh yes, daughter." The woman in the cell to their right smirked from where she lay draped in violet silk on a large brocade lounge. The area around her was furnished like a grand sitting room, complete with a small pianissimo in one corner. "It's a trait you carry in full measure. Perhaps you wish to entangle with that dragon trash next to you, since he is so eager?"

Hrelana's voice turned silkier and more beguiling. Faint mental tendrils wove around Tiers, enticing him to whatever his heart desired. Freckles tensed and hissed in his arms. Tiers pushed the tendrils away easily enough, but he took Nula's hand. <Persuasion Talent?>

<Through vocal harmonics, yes. It only works in close proximity, and even then, only for a short period of time. The glass usually inhibits it, but I disabled the vocal dampeners so we could hear them and they could hear each other. Let the circus begin.> Nula turned to the left, where a gentleman stood in a room crowded with shelves, a small desk, and a generously cushioned cot. "Well, Father? What do you have to say in response?"

The prisoner, the former Grand Count Nul, brushed off his gray silk waistcoat and fixed Tiers with a scrutinizing glare, assessing his value. Nula's dossier had mentioned that she inherited her Talent from her father. "Ah, this dragon is gold to you. Fascinating how that turned out. I suppose your mother was right when she said I ruined you."

Nula tilted her head. "And just how did you do that?"

Before he could speak, Nula's mother interjected, her round face curled in a snarl. Her voice was pure poison. "By taking up with one of those hideous flying beasts instead of keeping to his own kind."

"You of all people should appreciate the opportunity for scientific study," her father shot back, shaking his fist at the wall that separated the couple. His small spectacles quivered on his nose, and his umber face was lined with sweat. "It was an unparalleled opportunity to explore the effects of a rare union. I didn't expect the offspring to survive."

"Yes, but you should have asked permission first, instead of counting on rumors of my heritage to cover up our daughter's quirks."

"Such heart-warming devotion. I expected nothing less from the two of you." Nula clutched his hand. Her face remained stoic, but Tiers sensed the tumult of emotions shoved beneath her pragmatic focus. "Since I am apparently half dragon, instead of just carrying a few ancient traces of dragon blood, could you please explain how you repressed those traits?"

"We did nothing of the sort," her mother spat, her sandy skin flushed. She sat up and jabbed her finger at the glass. "It was an unsanctioned experiment, but once the deed was done, I wasn't about to waste the opportunity to observe the results." Her brown eyes turned calculating as she studied Nula and Tiers's joined hands. "Fascinating. It appears to have remained dormant until you met a dragon mate. If only I had a pencil and a notebook, this would be quite the opportunity for analysis."

"A pity that both are considered dangerous, Mother, especially for you." Nula swallowed, and Tiers felt her emotions rising within her.

Freckles gave a small mreow.

Tiers reached for her with the lightest mental touch and soothed what he could with his own peace. Her shoulders loosened, and she closed her eyes, slowly breathing in and out. After a moment, Nula fixed Nul Thredsing with a stare. She continued, "Father, it's apparent that you had a part in this. You must have some idea of how the experiment would continue on the chance I met a compatible embermate."

"Ah, yes." Nul rubbed his hands together with glee. The files had claimed Nul Thredsing was a specialist in sociology and psychology. "Let me think. The plan was for the dragon to be captured and held, and the two of you observed for any aberrant relational behavior. Once sufficient psychological studies had been performed, your mother would have overseen the heart transplant."

Nula stepped forward, her expression sharp. "How were you planning on keeping me alive?"

"Presumably, your heart would have undergone sufficient transformation, along with the rest of you. If not, we would have studied your remains afterward. All of that really isn't my department, you understand." He waved dismissively. "Your mother handles those details."

Nula's mother stood, brushing off her silken skirts, her expression disdainful. "Yes, those 'details' that fueled countless volumes of useful research for our cause while you frittered away your time at useless parties."

"Creating deals that made money, which then fueled your research!"

"Creating deals. A useful euphemism." Hrelana rolled her eyes. "As for the problem with the heart-bonding—ah, daughter, I see you need this information. Yes, you need it very much." Her eyes glittered. "How much?"

Nula raised her eyebrows. "How much of what?"

"How much is your life worth? After all, I hold it in my hands with this knowledge. You need a specific laboratory, and if you had found it, you wouldn't be here." Nula's mother folded her arms. "What are you willing to give me in exchange for its location?"

Tiers could sense the anger and fury threatening to burst forth from Nula. "For you? One hour in the torture chamber sounds fitting." She glanced at Tiers. "What do you think?"

Her expression revealed no hint of bluffing. Her emotions were mixed with grief, but only slightly. She truly was as ruthless as a dragon. Part of him hoped it wouldn't come to torture, if only to spare Nula the difficulties of such an action. The other part believed the world would be a far better place without her parents. He looked at his embermate and nodded. "I can arrange for the use of specific implements that humans have never experienced, including creative ideas with dragon fire."

Freckles gave a low, menacing growl, and a tiny flicker of flame spurted out his mouth.

"Very good." Nula gave each of her parents a final glance and a cold smile. "Have a good day." She and Tiers turned to leave.

"Wait!"

Nula didn't even turn around. "Yes, Mother?"

"One piece of paper and one pen. For one hour."

"Ten minutes."

"An eight-by-eleven-inch piece of white paper that can be marked with ink."

Nula sighed. "After you surrender the information for the secret facility, and it is verified."

"Agreed."

"I will inform the Lawless."

Nula put on her goggles and pressed her hand to the invisible entrance pad. Tiers took one final look behind him at the imprisoned scientists, kept in their far-too-luxurious cells while so many others fought a war that shouldn't have happened.

Anger burned within him. "If the information you give is incorrect, you will be tortured. By dragons."

The cat-dragon Tiers held against his chest spurted another flame in agreement.

The scientists' faces paled.

He turned and left the cell with Nula before the fury within him escaped and he tried to kill her parents himself.

CHAPTER ELEVEN

ANGER, GRIEF, AND FRUSTRATION battled inside Nula, twisting her stomach and leaving her mouth as dry as ash and her throat as raw as the words her parents had spoken. Not that they had been much of a surprise, except for the unfortunate news of her birth. A half-dragon, borne of scientific curiosity between a Pinnacle dragon and her father under the control of the Curious Intrigue.

Good thing she had helped take them out of power in the Scepter of Commerce. Grim satisfaction filled her.

She entered the code into the circle and stomped into the elevator, trying to force her feelings away. Tiers's hand in hers could only go so far.

"Well, that's one comfort," Nula said, staring at the recessed lights as the elevator ascended. "When my mother is executed, as I'm sure she will be, it won't be as if I've lost anyone."

"You could think of it that way." Tiers's voice was level, his emotions an unsettling mixture of compassion and rage. "Yet it isn't always that simple, is it?"

"How would you know?" She yanked her hand out of his and stalked out of the elevator, turning left to leave through the back door. "Are your parents despicable, self-obsessed, psychopaths who only wanted you for an experiment?"

"No." He was quiet for a long moment as they walked down the street. "Are we not summoning a groundcar, then?"

"I need to walk," she growled. Her mouth felt as though it was on fire.

"Understandable." He fell into step beside her, keeping pace as always. Freckles squirmed out of his arms and took off into the air with a hiss, his wings beating strongly. Before they could do anything, he flew ahead and vanished around a corner.

Typical cat. Only around when he wanted to be. She felt a twinge of concern but killed it quickly. Good riddance to him. It would be easier without an animal around to worry about.

Nula clicked her teeth and walked faster, her low heels loud on the pavement. The street traffic in the High Quarter was a casual affair, and she rapidly brushed past each window shopper and midday stroller, all of them unaware of how terrible they were. How terrible all of humanity was. And dragons. Everyone. Still, Tiers kept pace with her, his expression vaguely troubled. The fool. How did he think she would react?

"At least in my lineage, you won't face any condemnation for your mixed heritage or your spy work," he said. "My parents are alive and well. I try to see them every other month. They are one reason I've been able to maintain my role in espionage."

"Good for you." Something dark and shadowy emanated from her mouth. It had to be an illusion. Perhaps the sea breeze had blown smoke from the south factory district.

"I'd like you to meet them sometime."

"What, so they can be suspicious of me as well? So I can have my intentions vetted by yet another inquiry? No, thank you."

He sighed. "As I said, they wouldn't treat you like that. My parents have been involved with the Lawless as espionage agents for my entire life. They understand the life you've had to live more than most."

Her words came out clipped and loud. "You mean gray areas. Blood on your hands. Treachery for the sake of progress. Turning in people from both sides for the sake of the cause."

He grimaced "Yes. And I understand this as well, as you know."

Something in his knowing tone set her insides ablaze, giving her a target for her anger. "Yes. The blasted dragons attacking my city are partly thanks to you, right? Your failure to turn someone to the side of the Lawless?" Nula stopped and studied Tiers. His face was an unreadable mask. "Correct me if I'm wrong, but the protocol for failure to turn a potential asset is that they must be killed. Is it not the same for dragons?"

"It is." His eyes were golden slits of anger, and scales had appeared on his forehead and cheekbones.

"Then why is this dragon still alive? Are you incompetent?"

Tiers glared at her. "The situation was complicated. I had to adapt to the circumstances."

"Complications," she scoffed. "We all have complications. You've met two of mine."

"Who are also still alive."

"My parents are in prison! And they are there because I made hard decisions, handled the situation, and did my job. You didn't—"

A red-orange stream of flame swallowed the rest of her words. It narrowly missed scorching Tiers's hair, and instead melted the awning of a nearby sweets shop.

His eyes widened. Nula slapped her hands over her mouth. The transformation. She was half dragon. Apparently breathing fire was part of the package. Her heart drummed, and fear coiled in her stomach. What the ducus was she supposed to do now? What other traits would emerge? Would she survive?

Nula inhaled sharply. She needed time to plan, time to think of a way to break the news to the council. A future grand countess could not be seen spewing flames in public.

Tiers grabbed her hand. <We have to get you out of here.>

<Agreed.>

<Not so fast, traitor.> The voice was new and sharp with a predatorial edge.

A second later, a shot cracked through the air. A man walking in front of Nula fell to his knees, then rolled to the side and lay still. Nula whipped around, watching as a woman dressed in factory coveralls advanced toward them, her blonde hair threaded with indigo strands.

Not a human.

A dragon.

One of *the* dragons. The embermate of Tiers's fleetwing. The dragon woman sneered and gestured with her pistol. "Come with me, or more will die."

Nula raised her eyebrows. "No, you will. Do you think the Scepter of Commerce has no police force?" Even now, she could see plain-clothed and uniformed officers pushing their way over. The High Quarter had money, and that meant law enforcement was encouraged to be exceptionally diligent. It wasn't particularly fair, but fairness mattered less when a gun was pointed in your direction.

Another crack. The bullet whizzed past Nula's ear as Tiers yanked her to the side. His expression had turned from resolute patience to fierce protectiveness, with scales emerging along his face and other exposed skin. "Get behind me. Stay down."

"She has a gun. What do you think you are—" Nula cut her words short as she ran around the corner of a building, stopping to peer around the edge. She was a fool. Tiers had probably been treated with slatesheen throughout the course of his life. He was bulletproof in most situations.

But the civilians weren't. Even the officers had limited body armor, and they only wore it regularly in the Low Quarter.

The dragon woman aimed and fired. Tiers lunged to the side, grunting as another bullet bounced off him. He began taking measured steps forward. "Jylle, stop this."

"Why should I?" Her scowl deepened, and indigo scales surfaced on her skin. "I have nothing to lose. And you have everything to lose, don't you, Tiers? I can sense your connection to the human. It figures that a traitor like yourself would find your embermate in an equally weak woman."

Law enforcement ushered away the panicking bystanders, while more officers surrounded the dragons. One called out, "Stand down, both of you."

Jylle cocked her pistol and took several more shots. Another spectator fell to the ground, clutching his shoulder. Others dropped back. One officer flung a glass vial between the two dragons.

It shattered, and with it, Nula's heart. Yellow arsin gas, created specifically to take down dragons, filled the air. It didn't matter that Tiers was a diplomatic envoy whose presence was meant to promote peace between dragons and humans in the Scepter. She could understand the rationale. Contain any potential threats at all costs. But at that moment, it took everything in her not to rip every officer to pieces for daring to harm her dragon.

Because she was half dragon. And Tiers was hers.

She glanced through the smoky haze, trying to get a glimpse

of Tiers. As soon as the vapor cleared, the officers could lock Jylle in a cold, dark hole, but there was no way Nula was letting them have Tiers.

But as the breeze shifted the yellow cloud, she saw a figure standing triumphantly, blonde hair waving in the wind, and what seemed to be a bubble surrounding her. Nula swore thoroughly. The dragon had some kind of shield Talent protecting her from the gas.

Tiers had no protection.

Jylle bared her teeth in Nula's direction, then leaned over and raked her claws across

Tiers's chest, creating deep gashes. Nula froze in horror. What about the slatesheen? Apparently, it didn't protect from this.

Anger filled her, blasting out of her mouth in a burst of flame. To hell with the smoke. She was going to get her embermate.

Nula ran into the cloud, coughs wracking her body. She clenched her teeth and spewed the next cough out in another blast of fire that left her mouth raw.

Jylle looked up and smirked. "So, the frail human has some flames. Too bad the rest of you isn't as protected. Then again, I'll enjoy slicing your pretty skin to ribbons."

"Fireless leadstone!" It was one of the worst insults to give a dragon, bad enough that Jylle paused to glare at her. Nula grinned and opened her mouth, aiming another stream of fire at the dragon woman, but Jylle's bubble deflected it.

Another round of coughs ravaged Nula, and she fought to stay standing. Jylle stood and walked toward her. "Just for that, I'll start with your face."

Her clawed fingertips reached toward Nula. Nula stumbled back, trying to avoid breathing in the poisonous yellow fumes. She had to think. There had to be something she could do.

A sharp horn pierced Jylle's palm, and a screech like a neigh and a whining sawblade filled the air. Nula blinked. A massive four-legged figure loomed in the haze, its eyes gleaming points of blood red and the scent of sulfur emanating from it. And the spiky object it pulled out of Jylle's hand was definitely a horn, coated in some kind of black, sticky substance.

Her heart stopped, even as her voice struggled for words. "A… unicorn?"

Impossible. They were extinct. And in pictures in books, unicorns had never looked so deadly.

Jylle recoiled with a shriek of pain and anger, backing out of reach of the dangerous horn. The beast turned its nearest eye toward Nula. A curt male voice spoke in her mind. <Yes, I'm a unicorn. Yes, I'm real. Get yourself and your friend on my back. Now.>

A rush of adrenaline flooded her. Nula leaped to her feet and ran to Tiers, picking him up off the ground with a burst of strength unfamiliar to her. The unicorn followed her, kneeling down enough for her to roll Tiers onto the beast's broad back. She scrambled up alongside her embermate, wishing she knew more about horseback riding beyond what a few summer vacations in the Southern Plains had taught her.

Nula glanced behind her. "Unicorn-person, the dragon is trying to—"

His back legs kicked out, knocking the dragon woman to the ground and evoking a groan from Tiers. Relief spread through Nula. At least it meant Tiers was alive.

<Problem solved.>

<Why don't you kill the dragon?>

<Right now, we need to deal with the half-dead one on my

back. The psychotic one will keep. Hold on.>

Nula grabbed hold of his mane with one hand and Tiers's bloody body with the other. <Where are we going? How can I hear you in my mind?>

<You have shifter blood. It must have activated just now. And we're going to your house. Where else?>

<But he needs medical attention!>

<I'll be there, so you'll have it. Hold on!>

The unicorn launched into a full gallop, disappearing down a side alley and into the maze of streets in the Scepter of Commerce. Nula fought to stay on his back and tried not to look around her too much.

But she did see a certain cat-dragon flapping his wings above her and giving her a decidedly smug look.

Once this was over, Freckles had some explaining to do.

CHAPTER TWELVE

WHEN THEY ARRIVED at Nula's silver-gray mansion, Zilpath opened the door.

Damn.

"You have the worst timing," Nula announced. The unicorn stomped his foot on the ground, as if to emphasize her words. "Get out of the way, and let us in."

The old woman's fingers quickly swept through the air, her eyes flashing with concern. ~Not until you explain what is happening, young lady.~

"There's no time. We have a medical emergency. Move."

Zilpath glanced over the unicorn's head and saw Tiers's prone body. Her mouth tightened into fresh wrinkles. She stepped aside, and the unicorn immediately clopped into the front hall. Freckles flew toward Zilpath. She caught him in her arms with a scolding headshake.

<Get him off my back and onto a table,> the unicorn ordered. <Gather all the medical supplies you can. And if it matters to you, get me pants.>

"Pants? Why would—you can shift?" Nula slid off his back, pulling Tiers with her. Without the emotionally-charged adrenaline from earlier, the dragon's skin form proved to be quite heavy, and he quickly sagged to the floor. Apparently her dragon blood hadn't given her *that* much dragon strength.

A second later, the unicorn was replaced by a tall man with long black hair, dark olive skin, pointed ears, and a small silver horn emerging from the center of his forehead. And no pants or clothing of any kind. He knelt next to Tiers and lifted him into his arms, then fixed her with a violet-eyed stare.

Hadn't his eyes been red? Where had the smell of sulfur gone? What about pants?

"Where is your medical facility?"

She focused. "This way."

Pants could wait. They needed every second.

Nula made a few quick signs to Zilpath that sent the old woman running to another room for some kind of covering. Then Nula started up the stairs to the scratched-up table where just a few days ago Tiers had treated the injured cat-dragon with such care.

The unicorn set Tiers on the table with a dismissive snort. "This is the best you have?"

"I was a double agent. My parents would have been suspicious if I set up a full medical clinic on the premises." Nula pulled out the dented medkit. "Here's what we have. I can get more in a matter of minutes."

"We might not have those. His lacerations are deep." The unicorn opened the kit and busied himself with the sterilizing liquid, pressing it over his hoof-black fingernails, then handed it to her. "Get ready to help."

Nula coated her fingers with the liquid, her hands shaking. She pressed her lips together. None of that. It was only blood. She was twenty-eight and had served as a double agent during wartime for sixteen years, surrounded by soldiers and assassins who died every day.

But not Tiers. Not today, when they'd ended with an argument, and then he'd put himself in the line of fire to protect her and civilians.

The unicorn shoved a handful of gauze at her, his violet eyes intense. "Get his shirt off and press this into the wounds to stop the bleeding."

Nula grabbed a pair of scissors from the kit and started cutting. "Shouldn't we have done this earlier?"

"Usually, yes, but dragons can endure more blood loss than humans. Getting him out of danger was a higher priority." He pulled out a section of tubing and a syringe. "Will the old woman be back?"

"Yes."

"Good. She can take over for you so I can draw your blood."

Nula looked up, shock zipping through her. "What?"

The unicorn had tied a length of rubber around his upper left arm and was tapping various spots around the vein in his elbow. "I can feel the bond that's formed between you and the dragon. You're not fully dragon yourself, but there is some connection from the embermate bond. Mixing my blood and yours is the best I can do for the present."

Nula's mouth dropped open. "Mixing our blood? Why yours?"

He pointed to the horn on the front of the medkit. "Have you humans forgotten what this means?"

"That unicorn blood has healing properties? You didn't look ready to heal when you were stabbing the dragon. And unicorns are supposed to be extinct! You all died in the revolution over sixty years ago in Elotrin. You had a backward view of Talents as magic, and you tended to disregard punctuality."

The unicorn snorted. "That's all you know about Elotrin? A handful of stereotypes?"

"I've had other priorities. Our countries share a border with one treacherous trade route, and supplies routinely run late from the south. How are you even here?"

"I've been here for a long time."

"Why?"

"More questions can wait." All the unicorn's attention was focused on his arm and the syringe in his hand, needle aimed at his vein.

Nula paused. Half of her wanted to help him. The other half was sure she would only make it worse. "Can I at least know your name?"

He paused, swiftly inserted the needle, then carefully withdrew a small amount of blood. He set the syringe aside and patted the area with a square of gauze. "Lirome. Yours?"

"Countess Thredsing—ah, just call me Nula." Standing on ceremony with a naked unicorn shifter trying to heal her dragon embermate seemed a little foolish at the moment.

Footsteps sounded. Zilpath entered the room carrying a length of fabric, followed by a frantically meowing cat-dragon that leaped onto a side cabinet and studied Tiers intently.

Zilpath threw the cloth at Lirome and accompanied it with a few gestures, some of them quite colorful. Her friend never did mince words, but in this case, she was merely being observant. Granted her observations were direct toward Lirome's physical appearance and apparent lack of spouse.

Nula cleared her throat. "She says—"

"I know what she said. Elric's hooves!" Clearly an expletive of some kind, from the unicorn's irritated tone. He rolled his eyes. "Thank you Zilpath, but no, I'm not interested in being introduced to any of your apprentices. Please sterilize your hands." With a few quick movements, he wrapped the cloth around the lower half of his body, then turned to Nula. "Let her take over and come here."

Nula rolled up her sleeve. In a matter of minutes, Lirome had drawn a full syringe of blood from her. She pressed a bit of gauze to the spot and watched as he injected some of his silvery-red blood and hers into a small vial. "Are you sure this is going to work?"

"Absolutely not. Pray to Bonilus and his emissaries. But the procedure has worked in the past. With humans and … yes. With humans."

So with people other than humans. Who else other than humans? Other types of shifters?

Zilpath smacked her hand on the table. Nula glanced over to see her frantically waving toward Tiers's still body, her fingers flying through the words. -Very cold! No pulse.-

Lirome's eyes narrowed. "Check him."

Nula felt the dragon's wrist. Nothing.

Her heart raced. She pressed harder, then dropped his wrist and checked up by his throat. The throbbing of blood was faint, but there.

She glared at Lirome. "You said he didn't need to be treated right away. You said he'd be fine!"

Lirome capped the tiny jar and shook it. "No, I said he would endure longer."

"His pulse is almost nonexistent!"

"He's a dragon. Their metabolism slows down under severe injury. It's a biological mechanism you didn't need to know about." He withdrew a fresh syringe from the medkit, filled it with the blood mixture, and walked over to Tiers, his steps far too slow and careful for Nula's liking.

"Tie the rubber tube around his upper arm."

Nula did so. Lirome tapped various parts of Tiers's arm, each second lasting an eternity. She impatiently shifted back and forth, idly aware of the soreness in her feet from running away from a crazed dragon and jumping from a unicorn's back.

Finally, Lirome plunged the needle into Tiers's vein, emptying the syringe into his arm.

"What happens now?" Nula asked. "When does it start to work?"

Lirome sighed. "Give it time."

"Is there anything else you can do in the meantime?"

"Yes. I'm going to clean and disinfect his wounds." He turned to Zilpath. "Can you get me a freshly-stocked medkit?"

She nodded and paused, glancing at Nula. ~You should come with me.~

"No. I'm staying here."

A hand gently rested on her shoulder for a moment. She looked up into Lirome's face. Despite the lack of wrinkles or other signs of aging, his expression was as world-worn as Zilpath's. "You can go with her. You need to check yourself for cuts and abrasions as well."

"I can do that here. I'm not supposed to be apart from him." Nula's throat heated with anger. She'd wanted Tiers out of her way before, but she wasn't going to abandon him now.

"Your caution is admirable, but a half hour of separation won't kill you or the dragon."

She lifted her chin. "His name is Tiers."

"Yes. Fine. My blood will keep *Tiers* stable, and since you are half dragon, you should be able to endure thirty minutes apart. He will keep." Lirome's face grew weary. "Your emotions are exhausting me. Calm your rage, for my sake. Then you can return and help me carry your embermate to a bed."

"I don't even know why you're here. What are your intentions?"

"I just saved your embermate's life. That was my intention. Now, I need some time alone." He glanced at Zilpath. "Please, explain what you can to her."

~I will. And you will have to explain the rest, old man.~ She gave the slightest nod of respect. ~Let me know if you change your mind about one of my shop girls. It would be a shame to waste you.~

Nula shoved her. "Zilpath!"

A chuckle escaped Lirome. Freckles gave a rusty meow as he hopped over to Lirome and rubbed his scale-speckled face into Lirome's arm. "I will keep that in mind."

Zilpath gave a satisfied smirk, as if making the unicorn laugh was a great gift, then turned to Nula. ~Come. You could use some tea. Or something stronger.~

"Stronger."

Nula gave Tiers one final look. She ran her fingers through his dark hair, expecting him to open his golden eyes and give her a look of quiet mischief.

She swallowed.

He would be fine. Everything would be fine.

It had to be.

CHAPTER THIRTEEN

WHEN ZILPATH HANDED HER a tumbler of Glansmead whiskey, Nula knew she was in for a nightmare of a conversation. As if being separated from Tiers wasn't bad enough. Bearable, but awful. As though an invisible force had taken hold of her heart and now yanked at it with every beat.

She focused on the drink. Glansmead was the good stuff. Even nobles could barely afford it. Nula had no idea how Zilpath could, but whenever it came out, it meant she was in the mood to be pushy and difficult.

Nula stared into the translucent, golden-brown liquid. The real nightmare was seeing Tiers lying on the table and being unable to help him. It was almost as bad as the night Dayevid had been killed.

Her fingers tightened around the chilled glass. No, her former lover hadn't been killed. He had been murdered in front of her, while she had to watch in approving silence. The fool had been too passionate for the Lawless cause, too reckless for his own good. In the end it destroyed him, with generous assistance from the Curious Intrigue.

There wasn't enough whiskey in Sekastra to erase those memories from her mind.

A gnarled hand gripped her arm, and Nula looked up. Zilpath sat across the table from her in a small alcove in the library. The table was filled with books opened in the middle.

They were her parents' books. Favorite philosophical texts on the superiority of the intellectual elite to rule over the working classes and control the world.

Only now, they were coasters. Nula set her sweating tumbler on a section about the genetic differences between the socio-economic classes. Zilpath squeezed her arm again, harder. Enough of that. Nula yanked away, glaring at her friend. ~What?~ she asked, slipping into pidsyn signing. ~I'm not in the mood to talk right now.~

~If you don't talk to me, I won't let you back into that room to see Tiers.~

~Like flames you won't.~ Nula tsked. ~It's my damn house, my damn table, and he's my damn embermate.~

Zilpath rolled her eyes and sat back in the overstuffed chair she'd pulled over. ~He's your husband.~

~Embermate. Don't talk to me about husbands. After seeing my parents today…~

Zilpath swiped her finger off the side of her chin. ~Husband. Embermate. Either way, you care for him.~

~If I cared about him, I wouldn't have left him in the hands of that horse.~

~Lirome is one of the best physicians in Sekastra.~

Nula tapped the edge of her glass. ~What kind of physician complains about my anger?~

Zilpath gave a silent chuckle. ~Unicorns are soul empaths, and they don't take well to strong negative emotions. If they did, people would suffer serious consequences. And have.~

~How do you know so much about them?~

~Why don't you?~

Nula scoffed. "Because they're extinct!"

Zilpath raised her eyebrows and smirked. ~Lirome seemed quite real for an extinct race. Such a shame.~

~What, that he isn't making little unicorn babies with some lucky woman?~

~No. Well, yes, but also that he's still searching for his sister.~

Nula paused, taking a generous sip of whiskey to keep herself from shouting at Zilpath for being so blasted confusing. ~You need to start from the top.~

Zilpath straightened in her chair. ~I don't need to do anything, young lady. You are the one who strolled in here on a unicorn with a bleeding embermate after what I'm sure was a disastrous meeting with your parents. What happened?~

~Nothing.~ She leaned over one of the books. The page was filled with complicated biochemical charts. ~This was my mother's book. Or so I thought. As it turns out, not only do we have different moral polarities, we don't even share the same genes.~ Nula gripped the edges of a few thin pages and ripped. She crumpled the pages into balls and threw them across the library. Zilpath watched her, eyes hooded. Nula chuckled and gripped another page. "Want to try? It's remarkably therapeutic."

~She isn't your mother?~ Zilpath paused. ~So your mother was a dragon?~

~Apparently. One in league with the Curious Intrigue or the Pinnacle. It was a scientific experiment to create a half-dragon child.~ Nula threw another few paper balls around the room, then sat back in her chair. ~My mother didn't know about it until afterward, but they decided I would be the perfect experiment. Then I disappointed them by having dormant dragon blood. My father was terribly frustrated, as you can imagine.~

By the end of her tirade, Nula's throat had heated up enough that she didn't need to crumple up the pages. She simply spurted out a stream of flame and lit the paper on fire. The flames licked down until they reached her fingers, warming her skin. For a moment, a flash of blue pebbled her fingers. Almost like … scales.

"Scales," she said aloud, rubbing her fingertips together. "Is that what I'm becoming? A flaming half-dragon with scales? Great! I can explain that to the council when I explain the unicorn who rescued me from an insane dragon woman and thwarted local law enforcement."

Zilpath grabbed Nula's hands, squeezing them until Nula made eye contact. Then she released her hands and began speaking. ~You never obey those officers anyway.~

~Yes, but I was going to try for the sake of that spot on the council. A chance to be more than a double agent no one trusts and whose parents didn't want except as a specimen to examine.~ Nula sniffled. Just once. It must have been because of the smoke in the library.

Zilpath moved her chair around the table until she sat next to Nula. ~Nula Thredsing, what did I tell you the night I found you?~

Nula sighed. ~Zilpath, what does this matter?~

~You were wandering by the Four Corners temple, having just witnessed your parents kill someone for the first time. Witnessed in part so you could be held as an accomplice. So that you would have to stay in the family forever. That knowledge made you almost as upset as the murder.~

Her blood heated. "They had no right to force me into that. To raise a child into violence and draft them into a brutal organization of conspiracies and criminals, knowing the blood on their hands would taint them."

~And what in Lady Allandra's blessed name did I tell you?~

Nula sighed, fingering one of her braids. "That I might have been born to terrible parents and been given a terrible upbringing, but I wasn't worthless. That whether or not I could see it, I had my own value and destiny. And that you weren't going leave me alone to get messed up by my parents, because I had too many opportunities and too much power to sit around feeling sorry for myself."

~Yes. And I still mean that. And if your fool-ass parents couldn't see your value, then so much the better for me. Because I always did.~

Then Zilpath's arms were around her, holding her close, fingers stroking her hair. Nula relaxed, and burning, angry tears trickled down her cheeks. It was a safer outlet than setting her parents' library ablaze, no matter how tempting it sounded. Once again, the old woman's arms were a place that offered kindness and security along with the sharp, caring words she doled out with her withered fingers. Nula breathed in the worn cotton fabric of Zilpath's baggy dress and was home.

At least, as much as she could be, apart from Tiers. Odd how the embermate bond worked like that.

She needed to check on him.

"All right, I'm better." She pulled away from Zilpath, rubbing away the crusted tears and fabric creases on her cheeks.

Zilpath handed her a damp handkerchief. Nula opted not to ask why it was damp—her friend believed her spit cured a myriad of ills—and dabbed at a corner of her face. No matter how much she wiped, there still seemed to be faint bumps pressing against her skin.

Bumps across her cheekbones, to be precise. Which was one place Tiers's scales manifested when he shifted into his skin form with dragon traits still visible.

"Zilpath, can you see anything on my face?"

The old woman leaned forward, her brow furrowed. Then she raised her eyebrows. ~A little. Like something is trying to break through your skin.~

Nula rose to her feet. Enough wondering. They had a physician of sorts in the mansion. It was time to make use of him again. ~Would the unicorn know anything about half-dragons?~

~Yes. Lirome knows almost everything there is to know about doctoring and chemicals in Sekastra or Elotrin.~

The awe on Zilpath's face stilled Nula's drive for answers about herself and Tiers. ~Just who is he to you?~

Zilpath hesitated a moment before responding. ~Remember how I said I was a slave for many years until I ran away?~ She stood, shifting on her feet. ~Well, I didn't do it on my own. I had a little help.~

~Lirome helped you? But that was, what, twenty-five years ago? And he doesn't look a day over thirty, if that.~

Zilpath shrugged. ~After maturing to adulthood, unicorns age far more slowly than humans and dragons. They live two hundred years on average. Part of their special blood.~

~I don't remember that in the textbooks. I don't remember their eyes turning red or them attacking humans like Lirome did, either.~

~Unicorns have reasons for their secrets. They have often been hunted. And bad things happened in Elotrin during the revolution, things Lirome doesn't talk about much. Says it takes him to a dark place. But yes, he and his friend rescued me and a number of other slaves. In return, I became one of their contacts in Sekastra. Met his sister too—she's a feisty one. When the war started, I joined the Lawless. Lirome and the unicorns hid, although I'd see him and his friend around sometimes, his sister not as often. But when she disappeared, Lirome showed up again. Zilpath patted her heart with her fist. ~Empathy bond of some kind.~

~What about his friend?~

~Disappeared too, in a sense. A good man, that one, but a hopeless romantic.~ Zilpath's face turned to a mixture of sad and sour. ~But you'll have to hear the rest from Lirome. You seem to be back to your old, cold-blooded self now.~

Nula grinned. "We'll have to walk back up the stairs. I hope your old bones can take it, because I'm not carrying you."

Zilpath's eyes glinted. ~I may have the useless Talent of knowing where I am in respect to the four directions, but I can still find a switch, even in this cave of a house.~

"Good. You can use it to fend off the evil dragon woman."

~My thoughts exactly.~

Nula laughed and grabbed the decanter of whiskey and a few tumblers. She needed to see Tiers, and she needed more answers. A little drink helped loosen any tongue.

Even, she hoped, a unicorn's.

CHAPTER FOURTEEN

AS IT TURNED OUT, healing Tiers had taken more out of Lirome than Nula had realized. When she walked into the room, he was slouched in a chair, leaning back against the cabinets lining the wall. He'd managed to find some pants, although he was still shirtless. Freckles was curled up in his lap, making a raspy-metal purr. The cat-dragon looked up as she entered, then gave a little nod to himself and shut his green eyes again.

"I see how it is. Loyalty when you choose." Though it was obvious the unicorn and cat-dragon had some kind of preexisting relationship.

She set the tumblers and decanter on a chair and walked over to Tiers, breathing in his sharp, peppery scent. His chest was wrapped with a thin layer of bandages. Far too thin, it seemed to her, though she was hardly a medical expert. Nula gingerly pressed two fingers to the side of his throat and watched his chest rise and fall. His pulse and breathing seemed normal. Relief washed over her.

"Yes, he's alive. I am slightly competent," muttered a voice from behind her.

She didn't bother turning around. "Considering how you were sleeping on the job, I had a few doubts."

"The folly of the young to dismiss sleep." She heard the chair legs hit the floor and footsteps as he walked over. His straight black hair fell in tangles past his shoulders, and his violet eyes were weary. "He's your embermate. If you weren't protective, I'd be suspicious."

Nula turned and faced Lirome with her arms folded, fixing him with her firmest stare. "What of it, then? I learned today that I am half dragon. What does that mean?"

He was silent for a moment, his face contemplative. Nula was tempted to ask again, but a nudge from behind her silenced the notion. Zilpath had made it up the stairs and was being her usual meddling self.

At last he spoke, slowly and carefully. "Well, it explains how you could hear my thoughts. Only shifters can hear each other within line of sight. Also, as a half-dragon, you should carry some dragon traits, but not all. From the way your throat lights up, I hazard that you can breathe fire. Since you couldn't carry Tiers up the stairs by yourself, it seems you haven't gained as much dragon strength. You reacted to the arsin smoke in the High Quarter, so it appears you have some dragon parts in your respiratory system, which bodes well for the open-heart surgery."

Nula stifled a flinch at the word 'surgery.' "So the surgery is possible?"

"Not only possible. Necessary. There may be other dragon characteristics that surface as a part of the need to be bound. Scales, for instance."

She pressed a hand over her heart. "The surgery won't kill me?"

Lirome shook his head, moving to check on Tiers's bandages. "Your body is altering so that it won't."

Relief filled her. "Can you perform the surgery, since you know so much?"

He fell silent again. After a few seconds, he said sadly, "I wouldn't recommend it."

A heavy weight sank into Nula's stomach. Who was he to deny her? She stepped closer to the unicorn, hands on her hips, using her Talent to assess him. Odd. His value tasted tarnished, incomplete. Somehow, this only fueled her anger. "Why not? What is missing?"

The unicorn's violet eyes flashed. "My sister, Maira."

"And how is she important?"

Lirome's expression remained stoic, but a wave of something furious and powerful smacked into Nula, pushing her back into Zilpath. The old woman stumbled and shook her head disapprovingly. ~I told you: unicorns are sensitive, this one even more so. You have to watch your feelings.~

Nula clenched her teeth. "I was under control."

"As much as a flooded dam, ready to burst," Lirome said. He glanced at Zilpath. "Can this conversation wait until after she spends time with the dragon? Even if they can't be heart-bound, at least after a day of healing they could mate and remove some of the tension."

Zilpath snorted. ~You would think so, but she doesn't work that way.~

"Gods. She should. I could use the break."

Nula let out a long, slow breath, trying to keep her voice level. "Would you two please tell me what the flames is going on?"

Lirome and Zilpath stared at each other, each daring the other to speak first. Then Lirome sighed and rubbed his forehead. Freckles gave a questioning mewl and flew into the unicorn's arms, burrowing there. The cat-dragon's action increased Lirome's value by at least ten percent. The creature must have a way of calming emotions.

At last, Lirome spoke. "My people are political refugees in Sekastra. My sister is especially important to our kind. She was captured during a tumultuous time in our home country, Elotrin, and was instrumental in the revolution which overthrew the kingdom sixty-three years ago. Over the course of a decade, our herd traveled here. We have kept secret ever since, but when the war started, Maira had been driven to help the Lawless. During one excursion ten years ago, she was captured, along with her chief mate."

"So why is your sister necessary for Tiers and me to get the heartflame surgery?"

Zilpath turned and stared at Lirome expectantly. Apparently, this was a secret the unicorn held close to his chest, a secret he kept even from a close friend. If he had close friends.

His jaw worked. "She's a healer. I can treat people expertly with my years of training and study, but her abilities advance far beyond that. It is her Talent. An incredibly powerful Talent. Unicorn blood already has healing properties, but Maira is special. Almost miraculous, one could say. I would trust her with your situation far more than myself. After years of searching for her, I suspect the Curious Intrigue has her in some secret facility."

A secret facility. Nula tapped her fingers against the table. "I assume they would want to use her exceptional ability in one way or another."

Lirome's face darkened. "Undoubtedly."

Zilpath glanced questioningly at her. Nula met her gaze, nodding in agreement. The secret Curious Intrigue healing facility, which hid at least one of the dragon attackers from the Pinnacle. Possibly two, if Jylle had gotten away.

For once, something was going right. Nula turned back to Lirome. "As it so happens, we're tracking a pair of rogue dragons in the city."

"Yes, I know of them."

"Good. We believe one of them is in this secret facility, and the other might have gone back there after you attacked her."

"If she made it. I kicked her hard." Lirome smirked. "What are your plans to locate this facility?"

Nula pressed her lips together. It was time to put her cards on the table. "Today Tiers and I visited my parents in prison. I arranged a deal with my mother to get the location of the facility. I'll need to contact Lawless officials to ensure she keeps her end of our bargain, but it should give us what we need."

"I must go there." He stared at her intently. "I have to release my sister in person."

"I'm not staying behind either. And you are welcome to come. You get your sister, we get the dragons, I get the credit I need, and Tiers and I get the surgery. After that, you can go on your merry way."

"Deal."

"Good."

Not a moment too soon. The reconciliation ceremony was in four days. She clicked her teeth, looking at Tiers.

"How long will it take him to get better? He needs to come with us. A half hour apart wasn't terrible, but longer?"

"Longer would be ill-advised. Fortunately, the mixture of our blood boosted his natural healing." Lirome set Freckles on a chair, then sterilized his hands. He walked around the table examining Tiers's wounds beneath the bandages. "I would say two days, and he'll be ready."

Nula pursed her lips. Two days was incredible, considering the depth and severity of his wounds. But she also knew that two days meant losing valuable time hunting for the facility. Maybe she could go without him. The idea bothered her, but it wouldn't be the first time Nula had ignored her feelings for the sake of progress. "All right. I suppose he will stay here?"

Lirome raised his eyebrows. "Yes, with you by his side for the entire duration. The estimate I gave you was predicated on proximity to his embermate. Without you, it will take him far longer to heal."

"So my instincts were right."

The unicorn nodded. "Yes. The half-hour separation was necessary, but I wouldn't recommend even that short of a time apart. Believe it or not, your very existence is necessary for his, and his for yours. You'll need to get used to that fact."

"But how? What scientific reason is there for my presence helping him heal?" Not that she minded staying close to Tiers. A part of her craved it. But there was so much to be done. She couldn't indulge herself when a plan was finally in place to end this.

"You forget, Nula, that we live in a world of magic and spirit as well as scientific progress. We unicorns factor that into all our healing methods. The dry-minded dragons in this country have limited your knowledge." He sniffed. "Now, if you would call some of the servants in this mansion, we can move Tiers to your bedchambers to recuperate. And then I am going to avail myself of a few more items of clothing and that whiskey you brought."

Zilpath's fingers began swiping at the air. ~Have you finally acknowledged that Sekastran liquor can taste good?~

~Never. But I'm running low on sterilization fluid.~

The old woman huffed, but her eyes twinkled. At a glance from Nula, Zilpath left to find two trustworthy servants.

An orange streak of fur flew across the room, and Nula held

out her arms just in time to catch it. The cat-dragon nuzzled her face, then settled against her chest and closed his eyes.

Nula snorted. "And here I thought you had forgotten about me."

"He never forgets, he only chooses his way." Lirome mock-glared at the cat-dragon. "I might have found him many decades ago, but that creature has a mind of his own. I hadn't seen him for weeks, and then he disturbed my work. You owe him your life. He wouldn't let me rest until I came to you."

"Really?" Nula glanced down at the cat-dragon. "I guess we are even now, considering we hit you with the groundcar."

"If that is what happened, he meant for it to happen that way."

"I see."

The servants entered the room, ending the conversation, which was fine with Nula. After a day of unexpected knowledge, she was ready to rest. After that, she would have to get creative about how to work around her healing embermate.

Thankfully, she had a large bed.

CHAPTER FIFTEEN

<YOU HURT HER.> The voice echoed through the shadows around Tiers. He stood in a fathomless place, alone and chilled to the core. <You, your shot-brained embermate, and that disgusting unicorn almost killed her.>

Yaron. His former fleetwing lurked in the shifting darkness. Tiers swallowed. <The last I remember, your precious embermate was trying to kill mine.>

Two glowing eyes gleamed in the darkness. <That pathetic human? She is nothing to you. No bonding has taken place. Jylle and I are joined unto death and beyond. Would you wish death upon your old friend?>

The mocking words held a trace of sadness. It squeezed Tiers's heart, even as he tried to push it away. Yaron had always been an excellent manipulator. <Maybe I should. She tried to kill me. Your feelings are false.> He shifted to his scale form, feeling the security of greater strength and mass. His eyes saw more clearly through the shadows, detecting the orange scales of his estranged friend.

<She wouldn't have killed you. Wounded you terribly, yes. But where I am, you would have healed swiftly. Faster than relying on the work of that foul horse. You wouldn't be stuck in this place if

you'd surrendered.>

<You would nearly kill me in order to save me?>

<Yes. You still have time to correct your past error.>

<Ah, so the error was mine.> Tiers breathed out smoke. Yaron always turned the blame on someone else. Yet, if the unicorn had indeed protected Nula and taken them both to safety, then he was already a welcome friend. His years in espionage had taught him to recognize allies quickly and discard traitors just as fast.

Except for Yaron. Somehow, Yaron always escaped. Tiers remembered Nula's accusing stare when she confronted him about his failure to kill Yaron. Some might have called her words harsh, but Tiers knew protocol as well as she did. From the haunted look in her eyes, she had been forced to personally carry out the policy. But he hadn't been able to do it, because he somehow imagined his old friend finally seeing the truth. Coming over to his side.

But all this time, Yaron had thought the same thing. And now the stalemate was prolonging the struggle and harming others.

There was no other solution. He had to be killed.

The resolution sank deep within Tiers, building an impenetrable wall around the part of his heart that protested his friend's fate. The wall rose, brick by brick, each one a wasted opportunity, sealed with the blood of the many Lawless and civilians that Yaron had killed over the last twelve years.

The only thing that remained was the last, twanging strand of the bond between them. It wasn't enough to track down Yaron or provide any useful intel, but it was enough for Yaron to invade his mind, just as he was doing now. He had always been outgoing, pushy, trying to force his views on others. At one time, Tiers had relished any opportunity to prove Yaron wrong, appreciating how his friend's chattiness had given Tiers the chance to collect information.

No more.

He visualized the strand, thin as spidersilk, a dividing line in the shadows. Tiers opened his mouth, ready to snap the line. Kill it forever.

<No!>

Yaron slammed into Tiers, clawing at him just as Jylle had done in the world outside. Tiers had held back from a frontal attack on Jylle out of respect for Yaron, allowing her one final chance. At that moment, Tiers had been willing to sacrifice Nula for the sake of this sickening bond, this impossible hope that his friend could be restored. And after all she had endured during that horrific confrontation with her parents…

She had sacrificed more in three days than Yaron had in a lifetime. If part of it was to benefit herself, Tiers could respect that. She had never tried to hide herself beneath emotional manipulation.

And he'd failed to protect her.

Never again.

Rage filled Tiers. He roared and lashed out at Yaron, ripping at his throat, feeling the blood and tendons shred beneath his jaws. The other dragon stumbled back with a pained bellow. <Tiers!>

<You are nothing to me, Yaron Flamestriker.> Tiers recalled the last words of the fleetwing renunciation vow. The ones he had never dared to speak. <As in mind, so in body. Your death comes.>

With that, he cut the thread.

All was darkness, drowning beneath an endless flood of pain at the final rupture.

Tiers gasped for breath, and his eyes snapped open.

Something held him down. He thrashed against it, pushing himself up. He couldn't drown. He couldn't do that to Nula, to the mission. To himself.

"Hey! Tiers, you're safe. I'm here."

He breathed in deeply, inhaling the scent of wheatsimmer. He blinked and focused his eyes enough to see the deep brown arms that gently but firmly held his own.

Nula Thredsing. His embermate.

She was alive.

He relaxed back against the headboard. Her bed, in her bedchambers, the walls decorated with tapestries of landscapes. To mimic the feeling of windows, she'd said, since she couldn't risk real windows. Too vulnerable.

"Tiers? Are you all right?"

He turned and looked at her. She wore a loose top and trousers, her braids pulled away from her face with a deep yellow scarf. Her clear gray eyes studied him with a mixture of relief and consternation, and her full lips were slightly parted.

She'd never looked more beautiful. All he wanted to do was drink of those lips and never stop.

Drink.

He swallowed and coughed. His mouth was as dry as a desert. "Can I have some water?"

"Yes!" Nula scooted down the bed and grabbed a glass of water from a side table. "I had everything prepared for when you would wake up."

"I can see that." Tiers drained the glass quickly. There were four tables lined up on her side of the bed. One was filled with various bottles of liquid and pills, one held a half-eaten tray of food, and two were filled with stacks of papers, books, documents, and a clipse-mirror. "You've changed the decor."

She gave him a smile that managed to be both sheepish and defiant. "If I was going to have to lay next to you for a few days, I was going to get some work done."

"A few days?"

"Two, to be precise. It's the evening of the second day."

She reached for his chest. Tiers caught her hand instinctively. "What are you doing?"

"What I've been doing every eight hours since Lirome showed me how: checking your bandages. Or what's left of them. Between your healing and that violent wake-up, there isn't much left. Bad dreams?"

"Yes. I killed Yaron." The words slipped out before he could stop them. Something in Nula's tone and their intimate situation made speaking easier. "In my mind, I mean."

She tsked as she nimbly felt the few strips of cloth wrapping his bare chest. "Well, I suppose that's one dragon down."

"At least in terms of our bond. It's … gone. The last thread."

Nula studied him closely. "Oh. I didn't realize you were still in contact with him." She paused. "But we each have our secrets."

He sensed the hurt in her tone and remembered how much she had willingly surrendered, while he clung to a hopeless cause. "Nula, I'm sorry. You were right. I should have broken the bond and killed Yaron long ago. You've given up so much, and here I am, a coward who refuses to face this one hardship."

She pressed her lips together, her fingers hovering above his bandages. Her face was stone. "I should remove these and see how you've healed."

"Yes. Good."

He watched as she lightly tugged at the first one, then carefully unwrapped the length of cloth, refusing to meet his eyes. Quiet, for once, but not out of concentration.

Out of grief.

"His name was Dayevid. He was my primary resistance contact when I was twenty. We became involved. We both tried to pretend it wasn't serious. There are no secure relationships in our line of work." Her hands shook slightly, but she kept unrolling the bandages, revealing scarred skin. "And yet, when the Curious Intrigue brought him in as a rebel, and I stood in the execution room, looking into his eyes, my heart betrayed me. Almost." Her voice grew bitter. "I learned. I acted as if Dayevid held my heart in that interrogation room. And when they pulled the trigger, it killed my last feelings as well."

Each word, raw with emotion, pierced his heart. Tiers reached out and tentatively stroked her knee. "Your parents really did execute him."

"Oh, the weapon wasn't in their hands, but they gave the order, and we were all in the room. Dayevid's death was quite a thrill for the Curious Intrigue. Only, I knew he'd given himself up for a reason. His death was part of a larger mission that later crippled one of the Curious Intrigue's plots." She finished rolling the last bandage, placed it on one of the tables, then took a clean rag from a bowl of herb-speckled liquid. "All that to say, I understand sacrificing what you want for the greater good. I also understand wanting to cling to something outside of that. It's the curse of espionage. Always lying, never honest. Never real."

She began to clean the bandaged area, her face a mixture of pain and stubbornness. Tiers's voice was thoughtful. "That's why you want to be on the council. So you can be done with this life."

"Thredsings have been on the council since the founding of this Scepter. I want to fix what my parents have done to the family name." Nula paused, her voice quieting. "And … yes. I want to be free."

Tiers covered her hand with his, stilling her actions. "I want that for you as well, Nula. I want that for myself."

"You do?" She glanced at him, her expression almost shy.

"Yes. With you." He gave her a sly smile. "Well, as much as we can. Can't let all of those espionage contacts go to waste."

She grinned, her eyes lighting up. Fewmets, she was beautiful. "I do like a man who won't waste good spy connections."

"I like you."

Nula's skin began to shift beneath his touch. Tiers pulled his hand away from hers. Fine turquoise scales glimmered against the warm brown skin on the back of her hand. She raised her eyebrows.

"So those are what the fuss and ripples were about." Nula eyed him speculatively, her gaze tinged with desire. "When you allow your scales to show in skin form, where do they emerge?"

Tiers's chest tightened, and heat rushed through his veins. "Many places, some of them quite … sensitive. I could tell you, or, since my touch seems to have this effect on you, I could … show you."

"I think showing me would be far more memorable." She threw the washcloth aside and leaned over him, her fingers slowly trailing down his chest. Drawing forth his own scales, even as her touch made his breath quick and shallow. "After all, I need to embrace my dragon side to prepare for our heart binding."

Tiers's mind raced with questions. Had they found the facility yet? Would sex be safe? He managed to curb his desire enough to utter a few words. "Nula. Dragons, in passion, get very heated. It might not be—"

"I'm already breathing out and touching fire without getting burned." Her fingers continued their pleasurable pattern. "So please, get very heated."

The last boundary vanished. He pulled her down against him, slipping his hands beneath her shirt and tracing over the curves where scales emerged on a dragon woman. She gave a soft moan and closed her eyes.

Embracing her was all he needed. Relishing, cherishing the beauty of her. Inhaling her sweet scent of wheatsimmer liquor. Pressing in close, even as she whispered in his ear and clung to him fiercely. Capturing her mouth with his as flames danced between them. Claiming each other, even as his heartflame thundered, anxious for the final joining that was to come. But for now, this was enough.

This was everything.

At last, they lay in each other's arms, relaxed and still slightly breathless. The sheets lay in singed rags around them, the mattress scorched beneath them. Nula gave a low chuckle against his throat. "I needed a new mattress anyway. At least my bedframe is made of iron. I should send someone out to buy flame-proof bed sheets. Where could one find something like that?"

"Nowhere in a human city." He kissed the part in her hair. "But my parents would give us some."

She leaned up a little, giving him a skeptical look. "Your parents? Really?"

"It's a traditional embermate bonding gift in dragon culture. My parents worked in textiles before the war. They're quite skilled."

"How practical of them." Nula traced a circle on his torso, evoking a growl from his stomach. She chuckled again. "I guess you've found your appetite?"

"A few mountain grazers would be delicious. Or whatever the equivalent is for this kind of stomach."

"I agree. I didn't realize a tumble could be this … energetic." She eased away from him and off the bed, walking to a bronze keypad and pressing in a pattern. She didn't bother to pull on a robe, which was fine by him. She could spend the rest of their time together unclothed without complaint from him.

A high-pitched, mechanical screech interrupted his musings.

"Yes, my lady?"

"Send up a full meal, enough for four people. Generous portions. Include plenty of water and some of the best wine."

"Right away, my lady." The voice paused. "My lady, there is a message for you from the Scepter of Commerce council. Would you like me to read it?"

Nula's lazy expression quickly vanished, replaced by anger and anxiety. "Yes. Now, please."

"Very good, my lady. It reminds you that you have only two days to handle the dragon problem, and that if you are serious about this, you should be mindful of the disappearances taking place in the Tolyon shoreline district. If you are not committed, they will find someone else to serve on the council."

Tiers sat up on the bed. The message was surprisingly direct for humans.

Nula curled her hand into a fist. "Thank you. Send up the food, please."

She pressed a button, ending the conversation, and shook her head, glaring at one of the tables. "Who do they think they are?"

"Well, I don't think the table will have the answer." Tiers eased off the bed and walked over to her. "Whatever it is, you are more than capable of handling it. And you have an administrative master and dragon in your corner. I want to take the rogue dragons down as much as you do. Then, you will be a grand countess. I will stay and run Lawless espionage from here."

She glanced up at him, surprise erasing her anger. "You mean that, don't you?"

"Yes."

Nula sighed and leaned against him.

He held her close, anticipating the end of Yaron's days.

The time had come.

CHAPTER SIXTEEN

NULA CREPT DOWNSTAIRS, listening carefully for any untoward sounds. Not that she expected any. But she didn't want to be heard by anyone else either.

Was it silly to be sneaking around in her own house? Perhaps. But Nula knew Zilpath and Lirome were keeping their own secrets, and neither of them seemed interested in divulging answers to her questions. Especially not Lirome.

Listening to their conversation when they thought she was otherwise occupied was the only solution.

To his credit, Tiers didn't even blink when she told him what she was doing. He merely gave her an approving look and mentioned that the seventh step in the staircase had a slight creak on the right-hand side, then followed soundlessly behind her.

Apparently destiny had gotten one thing right about her future. She smiled, thinking back to their burning tangle in the sheets. But pleasurable experience had settled very little. Afterward, her heart had turned into a flaming coal, ready to leap out of her chest.

Very inconvenient, considering they still had to track down the mysterious healer and the dragon facilities in order to endure the surgery. Nula turned a corner and heard the distinct sound of nothing. A very particular kind of nothing tainted by the faintest sound of something swiping through the air. The only way she heard it was due to years spent in Zilpath's company.

Her friend was signing with someone, and it was likely a conversation that Nula would never be told about. Which meant it could be worth something.

Tiers touched her shoulder. <What is it?>

<Care to eavesdrop on a conversation?>

He smiled faintly. <I thought you'd never ask.>

They sneaked around, coming within line of sight of three figures in the drawing room. Lirome sat sprawled on the lounge, finally wearing an untucked white shirt, green vest, and black boots along with his pants. Freckles slouched across the seatback behind him. Zilpath sat opposite of them in a stiffly-cushioned chair, ignoring a full teacup that rested on a small table next to her.

Nula waited.

Lirome signed first. ~Are you sure no signs of Tyrius have surfaced?~

~Of course I'm sure. I would notice if a dictator from the past had suddenly reappeared and taken over High Command.~

The unicorn's mouth twitched. ~He was only in the court of the dictator. Besides, taking over High Command is something your protégé has already accomplished. There are more subtle signs, Zilpath. Unicorn mating bonds are different than those of dragons, but they are still very strong. And he was always a romantic, seeking love. That would have held true.~

~Understand, Lirome, half the airship sailors in the fleet find themselves in a woman or man's bed on furlough. It's still wartime in many parts of the country. None of them care to commit. Only a portion follow the edicts of the Four Corners as you and I do, or some other religious system or moral code.~ Zilpath raised her sparse eyebrows. ~You're sure Tyrius is a danger?~

~Or in danger. I don't know what they might have done to him. I had hoped, by this time, something would have changed for the better.~ Freckles flicked his tail in Lirome's face, and he brushed it away. ~When I find Maira, she will ask about him. He's her chief mate. She's going to want to help him. What should I say?~

Zilpath leaned forward, jabbing her finger at Lirome. ~You tell her that she is safe, that you are there for her, and that you'll sort out the problem with Tyrius together.~

Lirome snorted. ~No doubt. 'Driven' doesn't even begin to describe Maira. When she finds out something is wrong with Tyrius, nothing will keep her from his side. I'm certain you have no personal experience with such things.~

The old woman grinned. ~Why would I know about someone like that? I mentored a steamroller.~

Nula stifled a chuckle.

~Maira is more like a bolt of lightning than a steamroller. Chaotic. Brilliant. You never know when or where she will strike. Or who, for that matter. I certainly wouldn't have chosen Tyrius as her chief mate and mediator, but he excelled in the role.~

Nula tucked the information away in her mind. Considering that it was told in secret, she knew it wouldn't be easy to get the full story from Zilpath or Lirome. Truthfully, she didn't care. They had to find and eliminate the rogue dragons first.

But later, the unicorn and her old friend would have to explain themselves.

Tiers nudged Nula's mind. <Are you finished listening? Shall we reveal ourselves?>

<If you insist. After all, we are on a tight schedule.>

"This Maira sounds quite violent for a famous healer," Nula said loudly as she walked into the room. "Or should I say, infamous healer?"

Lirome studied her with narrowed eyes. "How much did you hear?"

"Enough to be both confused and enlightened. Like most parts of spywork."

Tiers cleared his throat. "You did choose one of the most visible rooms in the mansion to converse, so presumably you or Zilpath knew you could be eavesdropped on."

The unicorn glared at Zilpath. She only shrugged. ~And what of you?~ She studied Nula. ~What's happened to you? You've turned into a bolt of my prettiest fabric, with your shades of brown and those blue-green scales.~

"Fabric, hmm? I thought I was a steamroller."

Lirome observed Nula's scales with an approving look. "Good. I'm glad to see your dragon traits are emerging. Close proximity appears to be the best solution."

"Indeed." A smile tugged at Tiers's lips.

Nula found herself mirroring his expression, thinking back to his performance in bed. Very remarkable for his first time.

The unicorn stepped closer, giving her another scrutinizing look. "The scales are striking. Although, can you shift them away?"

"Not so far." She'd attempted several times, following Tiers's guidance. "We assumed it was due to the lack of heartflame bond."

"Maybe. There is also the possibly that, now that the scales have emerged, they will remain on the surface." Lirome held out his hand. "Do you mind if I check the state of your heart?"

"Don't you need equipment for that?"

"For in-depth examination, yes. But I have been a physician

for forty years. I have some intuition after all that time. And my empathy enables me to sense certain troubles."

Nula allowed him to place his palm over her heart. The unicorn closed his eyes and breathed in. She felt an odd sensation, as if a strange energy was gently enclosing her chest. The sensation was gone almost as quickly as she was made aware of it, and Lirome stepped back, his olive features lined with concern.

Tiers moved closer to Nula. "What is it?"

"We need to find the hidden facility as soon as possible. I didn't think this could happen."

Zilpath shook his arm until he looked at her. She signed, ~Speak plainly, you cryptic, horn-headed fool.~

"As a half-dragon, Nula's DNA is unpredictable. Its rapid emergence alone is noteworthy. But your heart..." Lirome shook his head. "It's almost as if—"

"What?" Nula snapped.

"As if you are turning into a dragon."

Her heart sank. Nula resisted the urge to sit on the lounge as Lirome's words spun in her mind. She certainly hadn't anticipated this turn of events. Could a dragon be a grand countess? Would she have to live among the dragons? Who would get her house?

<We will find a way.> Tiers's words were strong and steadfast in her mind. <You and I are used to bending systems to our wills.>

<Yes, but not genetics. That's my parents' department.>

Zilpath frowned. ~Are you certain, Lirome?~

"Of course not!" Lirome rubbed his forehead in frustration, his fingers lingering around his small, silvery horn that had suddenly emerged. "My initial words were an overstatement. Genetics don't work like that. There will always be traces of both dragon and human DNA. You may be mostly a dragon, but you will still carry human elements as well. It remains to be seen. This is all conjecture. We need to get to my sister and perform the surgery."

Tiers nodded. "So, what are we waiting for?"

Everyone turned to look at Nula. She blinked, then shook herself out of her thoughts. This was her mansion. Her mission. She called for the servant and Lawless agent she'd spoken to earlier, and the woman speedily appeared.

"Do you have the information my mother revealed to the Lawless?"

"Yes, my lady." The servant nodded and handed over a sheet of paper covered with lines of encrypted shorthand.

Nula nodded and took the paper. "Did you see this?"

The servant's expression turned from careful to flawlessly oblivious. "I'm sorry, my lady, but I was in the kitchen preparing the noonday meal. I saw nothing."

"You'll go far in this house." Nula gave her a smile. "And we'll be out for the meal, so please, take the rest of the day off and spend time with your family, and take as much of the food as you can carry."

"Yes. Thank you, my lady."

"You're welcome."

After the servant left, Nula turned back to the others. "We know the facility is near the Tolyon Sea shoreline. I will decrypt this on our way over." She turned to Tiers. "Naturally, the dragon diplomat wants a personal tour of all three seas."

"Of course. Water is my favorite substance." Tiers snorted smoke. "So much so, that I must encounter it properly armed."

~And obviously, you will take your favorite friend with you as a tour guide, since she knows the Scepter better than anyone else.~

Nula opened her mouth to refuse, then shut it when she saw

the gleam in the old woman's eyes. There would be no talking her out of this. As it happened, Zilpath did know the Scepter of Commerce better than anyone in the room and had her Talent of perfect direction on top of that.

Nula turned to Lirome. "You have your own method of getting there, I presume?"

"You'd be amazed how I can convince those around me to be utterly disinterested in my presence."

Ah yes, empathy manipulation. Less effective if you were aware of it, but civilians would have no reason to be. After all, unicorns were extinct.

She paused. "Care to use that empathy to mask an entire group?"

"If it fits into your master plan," Lirome said, smirking.

Nula shrugged. "None of this fits into my master plan, but I've learned to make new plans."

A questioning meow caught her attention, and she glanced at Freckles. She raised her eyebrows. There was absolutely no reason the cat-dragon should come along. "No. You can't come."

Freckles jumped from the back of the couch and flew straight at Tiers. The dragon caught him and found himself the beneficiary of many endearing cuddles.

"Curiously, he seems to have gained a lot of weight. And grip. Putting him down would be difficult."

"Of course it would be," Nula muttered. "Very well, then." They already had a dragon and a unicorn. What was one more animal? Perhaps the cat-dragon would be a good distraction. It had certainly worked for him thus far. She gave everyone a last, sweeping glance. "No one dies except the dragons. Get evidence."

"Agreed."

-Agreed.-

"Excellent." The coal that had been her heart flamed hotter. "Let's get to work."

CHAPTER SEVENTEEN

TIERS DIDN'T KNOW what was worse—the searing leaps of his heartflame in his chest or the fact that he was going to kill his old partner. The relief he'd felt earlier after clearing Yaron out of his life warred with the emptiness he'd left behind, an emptiness that cried out to be filled.

A hand touched his, the lovely brown skin covered with turquoise scales. <Are you all right?>

He shot her a wry look. <Am I that obvious?>

<Yes. At least, to me.> She pursed her lips, glancing behind them at the groundcar that held Lirome and Zilpath. <You forget: I've been where you are now, many times.>

Guilt coursed through him. <Yes, I know. You've sacrificed much for the cause.>

<At least I didn't have the mental bond with them like you did with Yaron. I can't imagine losing the closeness that we have.>

Tiers sighed and squeezed her hand. In his lap, Freckles squirmed into a more comfortable position. <It isn't that serious. Yaron and I weren't bound at the heart, obviously. There are two types of fleetwings. The Pinnacle prefers using dragons with innate embermate bonds, informing the pair that their bond is for

fighting, not love. This happened with Nightstalker and Ironfire. But those who have not met their embermates are connected with a tactical partner by blood-bond sharing. Adapted from unicorn shifters, actually.> He paused and glanced at her again. <You knew my feeling of regret?>

She shrugged. <Reading others is a cultivated talent in our profession. I've trained for years because it doesn't come naturally to me. Except in your case, for the most part.>

<Likewise.>

Nula's full mouth quirked in a faint smile. <I have to admit, it feels satisfying to be doing something about this situation. Taking action without having to compromise myself or my espionage life. It's one part I fear I will lose as a grand countess.>

<You plan on abandoning your contacts so quickly?>

Her gray eyes flashed. <Of course not!>

A chuckle escaped Tiers. <Since your husband has no intention of leaving his own career, I think you'll find ample opportunity to double-cross enemies and put them in their places.>

<Keep talking like that and you'll stir more of those intimate feelings from earlier.>

A rush of heat flooded him, intensifying the pain and need in his chest. Judging from Nula's gasp, she felt it too. They were running out of time, according to Lirome. They needed to find Maira and have her seal the embermate bond as soon as possible.

At that moment, the groundcar stopped by a large seaside cove. White concrete sidewalks embedded with polished stones and crushed shells bordered the road. The mosaics decorating the buildings were formed with shells and bits of polished sea glass. Ahead of them, the Tolyon Sea sparkled in the late morning sun, visible only in small patches through a crowd of people carrying parasols and a variety of sunshades.

They exited the car, Freckles curling up once more in Tiers's arms as Lirome and Zilpath made their way over. Lirome had shifted away all of his unicorn traits in order to blend in, which seemed to annoy him. Unicorns were creatures of authenticity, he'd said. Tiers couldn't help but think they'd make terrible spies.

Except for the fact that they'd managed to hide for three decades in Sekastra.

Nula raised her eyebrows. "How close do we need to be in order to stay in this empathic radius of yours?"

"Five feet is preferable so that I can manipulate their emotions." The unicorn's violet eyes darkened. "Although with this crowd, we will have to see."

"Do your best," Tiers said, turning to his mate.

Her scales were even more beautiful in the sunlight, twinkling and glimmering in a rich, vibrant reflection of the sea. A dangerous reflection. She'd draw too much attention.

Tiers gestured to one of the sunshades, the swaths of thin fabric attached to brightly colored poles. "There are other ways of disguising oneself."

Nula gave a brief nod of agreement. A moment later—and a quick exchange of dels with a merchant—and she and Zilpath both carried sunshades. Nula had also added a veil to her ensemble. Her nose wrinkled beneath the netting in discomfort, but it worked for the present. She and the old woman bent over the paper, studying the decrypted directions from the Lawless. After a swift exchange of gestures, Zilpath waved for everyone to follow her and entered the crowd, pushing through with her usual ferocity.

Tiers focused on the mission, preparing himself for what had to be done. He'd already killed Yaron once in the netherworld.

Finishing him in the physical one shouldn't be difficult. He felt Lirome's eyes on him. It didn't help that the cat-dragon was giving him the same look. "Are you reading my emotions?"

"Only because you're projecting them so loudly. I can barely focus on creating the disinterest field." The unicorn gave an annoyed huff. "How are your symptoms?"

"As bad as my embermate's," Tiers answered shortly, scanning the crowd.

"I'm sorry to hear that." Compassion softened his sharp features. "I wish the circumstances had been better. It seems the Pinnacle and the Curious Intrigue are doing to dragons what the Glorious Destiny and their kingdom did to the unicorns in Elotrin."

Melancholy filled his tone. Tiers glanced at him. "What is that?"

"Genocide for progress." The words were hard and bleak. "In the case of dragons, they attack your family relationships and bonds."

"What did they do to unicorns?"

Lirome's eyes seemed to flash red for a moment. The next second, they had returned to their normal violet color. Must have been a trick of the light. "They killed our descendants."

Alarm shot through Tiers. Why had the unicorns kept this information from the Lawless? Or was it simply above Tiers's station to know? Desire for answers overrode his focus on the present. He needed to know how this could affect his people. Most importantly, was Nula in danger? Before he could question Lirome further, the unicorn nudged him and gestured ahead of them.

Zilpath and Nula turned a corner down a narrow alley. Tiers increased his pace to follow them, but they had disappeared.

He gritted his teeth as his chest flared with worry. Absurd.

Under normal circumstances, he would have no trouble maintaining his composure. Of course the entrance was disguised. It was secret. Lirome's doomsday proclamations had shaken his focus. He took a few deep breaths to get himself under control.

They needed to solve this embermate issue soon.

"This way."

Nula's voice came from below. Tiers studied the ground, stepping carefully until he came to a part of the pavement that was cracked and depressed into a shallow hole. He placed his foot on the spot and fell forward, straight through the seemingly solid surface.

His pulsed raced. He resisted the urge to shift out his wings and instead forced himself to trust the destination. His arms clamped over Freckles before the cat-dragon had similar ideas to fly away. After a moment, the fall stabilized, and somehow, his feet were on solid ground once more. He stood in a circular room lit with electric torches in sconces on the walls. Nula and Zilpath stood in an opening that branched off into a hallway.

Nula's eyes widened. "Tiers, you need to move forward. Now."

He immediately stepped forward. A moment later, there was a rush of air, and Lirome landed on the ground right where Tiers had stood.

He tossed his black hair out of his eyes. "Interesting. I didn't realize the Scepters had developed anti-gravity fields."

"As far as I know, they haven't," Tiers replied. "I've been keeping track of the Scepters for years, and this is my first encounter with one."

Tiers shot a questioning glance at Nula, but she shrugged and shook her head. "I've not seen these either."

Zilpath gestured in agreement.

Lirome's face sobered. "Elric's hooves. It appears the Curious

Intrigue has stolen technology from Elotrin. The anti-gravity fields are a particular kind of device that uses sound frequencies and ambient magic to slow down the force of gravity. Sekastra shouldn't have enough magic for them to work. They must have adapted the devices."

Nula frowned. "I wasn't aware Elotrin even had advanced technology after the fall of your kingdom. The traders seem eager for Sekastran goods."

"Bits and pieces can still be found in the wreckage. Usually sold to the highest bidder." Lirome grunted. "We suspected this technology had gone north to Sekastra. This complicates matters."

"Indeed." Tiers recalled his own education among the Lawless. At the height of their power, Elotrin had been even more advanced than Sekastra, due to their mingling of magic with elements of spirit. Or that is what they claimed. Privately, most dragons believed that unicorns had simply found a way to access new and different energy levels. The idea of them tapping into the powers of the human soul or trying to use Talents as natural forces seemed absurd.

Tiers pushed aside his thoughts and focused on Nula, who was standing in front of a bronze door with intricate geometric patterns carved into the surface. His embermate had pulled her specialized goggles out of her purse and was flipping through different settings and muttering to herself. Next to her, Zilpath was signing rapidly.

Nula shook her head. "I tried that! There is no residual code showing on any part of the electromagnetic spectrum. No heat signatures. Nothing. And the surface is electrified. If I try to touch it, it zaps my fingers, the same as it does yours."

Lirome frowned. "It's likely coded to certain magic."

"You mean Talents."

"No, I mean the magic that manifests itself as Talents. Call Talents your magical signature, if you will. A Talent is how your body innately uses the ambient magic in our world. "

Nula rolled her eyes. "How does that even make sense? Talents don't work like that. We should just have you or Tiers break it down."

"No. That might set off some sort of alarm and endanger everyone." Lirome walked to the door and pressed his hand to the metal. He sighed. "Yes, it's triggered to react to any unapproved magical signature that crosses the threshold. And we all have Talents. We need another way in."

Zilpath shook her head. ~This is the only way in! What does it matter if we set off an alarm? You're a healer.~

"Oh yes, have the unicorn mend everyone's smashed pieces once we get inside."

Tiers sighed. This was getting them nowhere. What was the issue? Talents? He didn't make a habit of announcing his condition, but it seemed like the situation called for it. He cleared his throat. "I don't have a Talent."

All eyes turned to him.

Tiers shrugged. "Not all dragons in my generation were born with Talents. It's a genetic abnormality."

The unicorn's face darkened. "No, it isn't." He strode across the cement floor toward Tiers. "If I may?"

He held out his hand. Tiers, remembering how Lirome had read Nula, nodded and allowed the unicorn to touch his chest.

After a moment, Lirome smiled faintly and pulled his hand away. "You'll do."

"I'll do what?"

"This door is coded to respond to magic from certain Talents, which is why Nula and Zilpath can't touch it without electrocution. Since you don't have a Talent, you might be able to touch it without consequence."

Uncertainty knotted his stomach. Tiers shifted. "Might?"

"You won't know until you try. As Zilpath said, there is only one way in."

Frustration filled Tiers, rooting his boots to the ground. "But I don't even know what I'm supposed to be doing."

"Breaking down the door. You're a dragon. You should have enough strength to do that. Focus. Put everything you have into the task."

He shook his head, still trying to process this sudden information. "What if this doesn't work?"

"That's a possibility. But I think it is far more likely that you will succeed. My sister is somewhere in this facility, and she's the answer to the life-or-death situation you and your embermate are in. I wouldn't risk her life—or your lives—if I wasn't reasonably sure."

The calm strength in the unicorn's voice eased the tension in Tiers's muscles. This was the only option at present, and it seemed logical. He glanced at Nula. She nodded to him, her expression filled with solid trust. Heat rose in his chest. He handed Freckles to Lirome and walked over to the door. He focused on it as if it were Yaron, who had threatened the woman he cared for, who had lied to and emotionally manipulated him. And Tiers had allowed him.

He had allowed too much.

Tiers sucked in a breath and struck out, slamming the door with a sharp kick. And then a few more, each blow causing more wreckage. Just like the wreckage of the airship Yaron and Jylle had attacked when he first arrived. Another event he could have prevented if he had done his duty long ago.

<Tiers?> Nula's voice was calm in his mind, her touch soothing on his skin. <You can stop now. The door is dead.>

Behind him, Freckles gave a rusty mreow of agreement.

Tiers sighed, the action easing some of the tension inside him, and turned to Lirome. "Any magical alarms?"

"None at all." The unicorn looked slightly winded, likely from feeling the anger and frustration Tiers had projected. He gave the unicorn a faint, knowing smile, then turned to the dark opening that yawned in front of them.

Nula tsked and squeezed Tiers's arm, clearly ready to get moving. "Let me guess. Because Tiers didn't register on the magical alarms, any automated lights are also ineffective?"

Lirome nodded. "Quite possibly."

"Good thing we came prepared."

They all pulled out small torchlights, twisted the bronze pieces to activate the lighting device within, and entered the gaping cavity.

The hallway was made of cement blocks, and their lights revealed a shallow set of stairs carved into the cement. A flicker of panic passed through Tiers. Dragons hated being underground with no chance of escape. He had little idea of where he was, he hadn't made this cavern, and three others stood between him and the only known exit.

Perfect.

Nula grabbed his arm. <Can you see anything?>

<Only more of the same. And—do you hear that?> Tiers paused, motioning for the others to do likewise.

A buzzing, humming sound, like bees in a hive, came from somewhere in front of them. Tiers could also detect the slow dripping of water. The laboratory? He hadn't spent enough time in one to know for sure.

One person in their group seemed to know this technology far better than the rest. He glanced at Lirome. The unicorn's face was shrouded in shadow, his eyes keen and watchful. "Shouldn't you go ahead? After all, she's your sister."

"This place is sensitive to different kinds of Talents and magical signatures. Mine would be the first to set off any alarms."

"Yes, but why is that? And why did you insist that my lack of Talent wasn't genetic? How do you know that?"

"We need to keep walking—"

Nula spoke up. "No. There's no reason we should risk our lives for information that you aren't willing to reveal. Talk, or we stay here, and you can go in by yourself."

Tiers remembered the bleakness in Lirome's face during their earlier conversation, when the unicorn had mentioned the fall of his kingdom. "Your people have fallen. I'm only trying to protect mine from the same fate."

Lirome ground his teeth in annoyance, the sound echoing in the mostly-silent tunnel. The faint scent of sulfur trickled through the air for a moment before vanishing. Freckles purred reassurance in his arms. "Fine. What do you know about the fall of Elotrin?"

Tiers shrugged. "Not much. It was over sixty years ago. Not much is known about your country in general, and during that time, the barrier was in place. Someone with a force field Talent shut off your entire country from the outside during the revolution."

"We intentionally withheld or erased information about Elotrin from your history. We intentionally kept our technologically a secret. And the barrier itself was made to protect Sekastra."

"Who's 'we'?" Nula asked.

"The unicorns. And select dragons, all of whom are dead, as

far as I know. Except for one, and he is not on our side anymore." Lirome snorted. "Suffice to say that your Talentless condition is not natural, Tiers Sunscaler. It was done to you, probably by the Pinnacle or the Curious Intrigue."

"How?" Tiers asked. "I've never been part of experimentation."

"But you were a double agent within the Pinnacle during your formative years. Perhaps it was the SPU, the Pinnacle's Scientific Protection Unit. And before the fall of the monarchy, subversives could have already been setting the plans in motion. It could have been a potion added to the water or a steam in the air." Lirome sighed. "Talent removal was done to many in my country, slowly and gradually. It was the first stage of a coup that allowed the Glorious Destiny to take over our kingdom, and it very nearly destroyed the unicorns." Shadows crossed his Lirome's face, and then his expression hardened. "Before you broke down the door, I didn't know you had the ability to be invisible to magical security fields. Not all who had their Talents removed are able to be invisible to magical technology. Now that I know this, trust me when I say that as long as you go before us, it should neutralize any other alarms."

Zilpath grabbed his arm, making a series of signs. Lirome shook his head. "Yes, other traps are possible. However, the Curious Intrigue is too arrogantly secure in their new technology. The more secret and exotic it is, the more they disregard other safeguards."

"This is true," Nula said.

She met Tiers's eyes, her own revealing her misgivings but also the truth of their situation. What else could they do but trust Lirome? If they didn't get their embermate bond sealed, they would be dead soon anyway. What happened with his Talent could be dealt with later. It was certainly possible that an underground version of the SPU could have have corrupted dragon water supplies before the war.

But that didn't matter right now.

"All right, Lirome. But I would like to know more later."

The unicorn nodded. "I expect you will. You will need higher clearances from the Lawless first. But for now, we need to find my sister."

At the end of the hallway was an opening. No doorway, just another gaping hole with a faint light streaming through it. Tiers continued walking. A strange shudder passed through him, and he started at the odd sensation.

"What?" Lirome asked.

"I think I may have just walked through one of those magic fields you mentioned."

Lirome stopped. "Did you feel it earlier with the door?"

Tiers leveled a look at him. "I wasn't paying attention."

Irritation flamed within him. Tiers swallowed it, turning his attention back to their mission.

A few more steps, and the room opened up. It was a large, dimly-lit space about the size of the main hall in Nula's mansion. Tiers immediately scanned the area. There was nothing, save some slight rattling from cages along the walls. Creatures of some kind, perhaps food for dragons? The sharp odor of spoiled lemons filled the room.

In the center was a coffin-sized box of polished bronze and silver, wrapped in a complicated mess of tubes, wires, and dials. Four slabs of concrete surrounded the box, one on each side, each one an arm's length away. Handprints were embedded in the surface of the box. With a yowl of alarm, Freckles leaped from Lirome's arms and flew over to the box, landing on it and scratching at the surface. Tiny sparks of electricity flickered around his feet.

"Gods," Lirome spat. "That's what they've done to her."

"To who?"

He looked in disgust at the box. "My sister. She's in there. I can feel her."

Tiers blinked, not comprehending. What could this box have to do with anything? Lirome said his sister had an incredible healing Talent. Why would she be trapped in a box?

A box with tubes and wires to channel her Talent. Nausea rose within him.

A captive unicorn was the core of the Curious Intrigue's miraculous healing facility.

Chapter Eighteen

BILE ROSE IN NULA'S THROAT. Not because she was surprised by Lirome's accusation, but because she remembered seeing a document with a diagram of this exact set-up in her parents' files. She had only seen it for a minute. Her role in the Curious Intrigue had been more administrative, appearing as the public face of the Thredsings. Her parents had found her lack of scientific aptitude another reason to leave her out of their research. But that had not prevented her from sneaking into their rooms and peeking at their files. She'd committed some to memory, hoping that someday they'd be beneficial.

A part of her was relieved that the information she'd memorized was valuable. The other part felt sick at the idea that she'd been carrying information about draining a person of their Talent the way one would drain a battery. Nula shoved down the latter. There was no point in getting squeamish over issues like this.

She had to fix it.

Light hit her face. She blinked in the glare, barely able to make out the fast-moving fingers of Zilpath, who somehow managed to sign words around the torch in her hand. ~It isn't your fault.~

"I know it isn't. It's my parents' fault."

Zilpath's fingers stilled, and she looked at Nula suspiciously. ~Really?~

Nula sighed, tasting smoke, even though she couldn't see it. "Yes. I can't choose my parents. I can't choose my genetics. But I can choose what I do with my life. And regretting things I can't change is a pointless endeavor."

~Good girl.~

Zilpath gave her a triumphant smile. Damn it. The old woman still knew when Nula needed to speak the truth in situations. Being a double agent sometimes made it easy to forget who you were.

The fiery coal of Nula's heart burned painfully, feeling as if it would burst out of her skin. Nula almost wished it would, just to make the pain go away. She couldn't even feel affection for her old friend without agonizing discomfort.

Anger filled her. *She* got to decide when to feel things, not some stupid organ. She pivoted to face Lirome and Tiers. "Have the two of you finished? We have an important task at hand."

Lirome was examining the box, studying the various dials. Tiers had joined him, but he glanced up at her, concerned. She smiled back at him even while annoyance filled her. Did he think she was inept? Is that why he was concerned about her moment of weakness?

No. Tiers didn't think that. He cared.

Their relationship wouldn't be like her parents'. It wouldn't be a forced marriage of convenience constantly plagued with competition and mistrust. Tiers wanted the embermate bond. He wanted her, wanted to see her succeed. Which was why they were about to undergo a procedure that would knit them together, body and heart, in a very literal way. Tiers was gold, his value stronger and more vibrant when he was with her.

It would be fine.

Lirome gestured to the box, upon which Freckles had now sprawled, scowling as if he could glare the prison open. "We need to open this and free her."

Nula pushed away the nerves that prickled her skin and rummaged through her purse. She produced a small, battery-powered acetyl-cutter. "Good thing I made sure to bring this along."

Tiers nodded. "Good."

"Actually, I can't take credit for bringing this essential item." She glanced over at Zilpath and grinned.

The old woman held a second cutter in her hand. ~These are always useful to have around.~

Tiers flashed her a smile. "I don't suppose you have an extra?"

Zilpath shook her head.

Nula stepped to the bronze coffin-box and carefully knelt beside it. "How do you know that opening the box won't kill your sister?"

"She said it wouldn't."

"You're in contact with her?"

The unicorn nodded, a mixture of profound relief and worry on his face. "The coffin blocks most of my soul empathy, but we are twins. Our connection is stronger than most. Only chief mates among unicorns have a stronger bond." He placed his hand on the coffin. Tiny flickers of lightning arced around his hand, just as they flickered around the cat-dragon. "Because her Talent has been fused with electricity in the past, she is able to communicate through physical contact with this … contraption. She says we don't have much time."

Nula flicked on the acetyl-cutter. "Give me a few minutes."

"Try not to touch—"

The back of her hand brushed the surface of the box, and lightning arced around it, jolting her and sending her back on her heels.

Tiers raced over to her. "Are you all right?"

"Yes." Nula opened and closed her fist, flexing her fingers. "Although that was quite extraordinary. She's definitely alive."

"Yes, she is." Lirome grinned, a curious wetness in his eyes as he stroked the box. He seized as a bolt of electricity consumed his hand. His expression changed from fond to frustrated. "She wants to know what is wrong with you and how she can help."

Nula raised her eyebrows. "That's the point of getting her out of the coffin."

"I know, but she's insisting there is a faster way. She's as foolishly impatient as ever." Lirome scowled at the electricity sparking around his fingers. "And she's being very stubborn about it."

Tiers tilted his head to the side. "What does she think will help?"

"I don't want to—augh!" Lirome glared at the box. "It's an unnecessary risk, Maira!"

Zilpath grabbed his arm, then dropped it so she could sign. ~What is it? Whatever it is, now is not the time to keep your insights to yourself.~

"She wants to help you the way she's been forced to help members of the Curious Intrigue: by using their hideous system of healing that converts her natural Talent into electrical currents. She says it will be quicker than taking her from the machine and waiting for her to recover strength on her own."

Nula raised her eyebrows. "Is she right?"

"Yes. About that, at least. Instead of physical surgery, the process should sync your hearts and transfer enough genetic code for you two to be bonded."

Tiers's mouth dropped open. "She can do that?"

"I told you she was special. But not here. Not in this den of horrors. It's too risky!"

Arcs of electricity flickered around the box. Even without touching it, Nula could understand the gist of the response. "It seems she disagrees with you. I'm not sure this is the time to argue with the electrified unicorn of healing trapped in the coffin."

Another swell of heat squeezed her heart, and she stifled a groan. Beside her, Tiers winced, pressing his lips together.

Lirome looked between them, then his shoulders slumped. "Fine. Get on the slabs."

"What?" Nula's head snapped up.

"Get on the concrete slabs. One on each side. And get ready to put your hands on the coffin." He put both his hands on the bronze surface. Lightning sparked over his hands, and he grimaced. "This won't be fun."

His words spurred Nula into action. She swept past Tiers, moving to the other side of the coffin and climbing onto the slab. Her heart seared in her chest, and her breathing became shallow. She peeked over the top of the box and saw Tiers on the other side, his face a mask of determination.

His golden eyes softened ever so slightly upon meeting hers. Nula felt her lips curve up. For a single moment, all her fears vanished.

More electricity crackled and sparked around the coffin-box, turning the stagnant underground chamber into a maelstrom of light and shadow. Nula snapped her eyes shut against the blinding light and swallowed.

"I would say take a deep breath and relax, but that won't help you." Lirome raised his voice to be heard above the storm of currents.

"Touch your hand to the surface … now!"

Nula pressed her hand against the bronze box and bit back a scream as shattering arcs of lightning streaked up her arm and consumed her body. Every bone, every sinew, every part of her broke apart with the energy until she surrendered to the onslaught. Her heart split open, rent in two, as it had been doomed to do from the moment she set eyes on Tiers Sunscaler.

All was numb. Silent.

No room. No coffin.

Nothing except a slow beat in her ears, each throb endless seconds from the next, sucking away the very core of her existence.

But something new entered. Something strong and steady, suffused with cold logic and deep reserves of compassion. A force, a will, intensely focused and reserved, was laid open to her, enfolding her, joined to her.

Unto death and the reaches beyond.

Tiers.

My heart beats for you.

In the place with no sound, she chuckled.

Literally.

And suddenly, her heart—their hearts—sped up. All the weight and texture and feeling of the physical world pinned her body to the slab. Her eyes snapped open.

The world around her blurred with indistinct shapes and sensations. All too loud. All too much.

But through the fog of exhaustion and pain, her gut knew the truth.

Danger.

<Tiers!>

<I sense it.>

Their heartflames joined, each drawing strength from the other. Drawing hope from the other's desperate determination, borne of years of struggle and success at a brutal cost.

A dragon's roar filled the room.

Nula smirked.

It had no idea who it was dealing with.

CHAPTER NINETEEN

<GET DOWN!>

As one, he and Nula rolled off the slabs. Dragon flame blasted above their heads. She darted off, shouting at Zilpath to run. Hopefully the old woman was already gone. Her frail body and lovable defiance would be no match for the hatred fueling Yaron and Jylle. Freckles crouched low on the coffin, hissing, his ears flat against his skull.

<Nula, get out of here!>

<Oh, it's too late for her.> The voice mocked him. Tiers leaped into a fighting stance. A blow landed on his jaw. He rolled with the hit, ducking around more strikes. Yaron always did rush in for the kill.

The chilled calculations of combat descended on Tiers's mind. He welcomed it, even as he analyzed Yaron. The dragon's mussed brown hair and disheveled clothing showed his surprise, but otherwise he appeared to be fully healed. Tiers felt drained from the embermate bonding, but at least he was able to move, thanks to Lirome's mysterious sister. But there was no time to dwell on the unicorn in the box. He had to figure out how to throw his former fleetwing off his guard in order to kill him.

His resolve tightened. This time, Yaron would die.

<Tell me, Yaron. Where were you when we broke in? Off your guard? Lazy? Perhaps taking a stroll in the fine weather?>

The other dragon gave a sharp smile. <Yes, and that stroll involved abducting and killing a herd of humans for consumption.>

<Eating humans?> Tiers's mouth curled in disgust. <You have sunk to a new low.>

<Not compared to you. Joining with one of those pathetic creatures is abysmal. She will die along with you.>

<I think not.>

Tiers breathed out a stream of flames. Yaron backed up to avoid them, reaching out to brace himself against the coffin. Fingers of electricity arced through his skin form, and orange wings burst through his back as he took to the air. He sneered, <Unicorns. Inferior creatures only useful when contained and controlled.>

<Just like the Pinnacle controls you. But you will never see it.> There wasn't enough space in the small room for Tiers to shift into scale form and attack, but there was enough room for him to bare his wings as Yaron had done.

He flexed his shoulders, his wings ripping through the fabric of his shirt. Yaron flew toward the exit, doubtlessly trying to take the fight outside where he could fully transform and cause more pain and death.

No.

Tiers darted to the other side of the coffin and pushed off the ground, grabbing Yaron in midair and forcing them both to the ground. Sharp claws dug into Tiers's side. He jerked away, clutching his side while grazing the other dragon's shoulder with his claws.

They rolled apart. Tiers caught a glimpse of Nula in a standoff with Jylle, firing bullets from her pistol and casting flames from her mouth, all of which bounced off Jylle's shield Talent.

Yaron laughed. <You see? It doesn't matter if she breathes fire or if scales coat her skin. Your embermate is still a weak human.>

<Agreed, my heart,> Jylle said.

She advanced toward Nula. Tiers watched his embermate take a step back, then another, eyes wide with fear. Everything inside him screamed to protect her.

A blow sliced through the air behind him. Tiers dodged it, grabbing Yaron's arm and twisting it around, slashing at his wrist. His former fleetwing hissed in pain and yanked away.

<Nice try. But you didn't reach a vein. You've grown soft with the Lawless, Tiers. And now you will watch your embermate die.>

Nula was pressed against a wall, hopelessly firing bullets.

Jylle growled. "Is that the best you can do? Embarrassing. Killing you will prevent dishonor to everyone who carries dragon blood."

His embermate winced, and her lips trembled. But her hands were firm and sure on the pistol, and her gray eyes glinted with triumph.

<You will not have that pleasure.>

A unicorn horn pierced Jylle's gut from behind. She screeched and faltered, clutching the wound. Nula strode forward and fired three more shots at the dragon, each one hitting true. Not even slatesheen would protect Jylle at that close range.

Jylle crumpled to the ground. Her body fell still, her chest barely rising and falling. Nula stood over the fallen dragon with Lirome next to her. He was still in hoof form.

She grimaced. <Didn't you know? Unicorns *aren't* extinct. But they can be hard to see, especially when you're focused on killing someone.>

Yaron staggered sideways, bellowing in anger and pain. He whirled, claws lashing out at Tiers's neck and face. Tiers hissed and blocked his blows, but Yaron turned suddenly toward Nula, blasting her with flames where she stood, cornered.

She gave a strangled cry and dropped into a crouch, her shoulders twitching one way, then another. Lirome backed away from her with a nervous whinny. Nula tore off her corset coat, revealing two sharp angular objects pushing out from her back beneath her blouse. Another scream escaped her. Tiers's breath caught. It wasn't possible. She was only half dragon. But Lirome had said Nula's dragon blood was unpredictable.

<Abomination,> Yaron hissed, with another stream of flames.

Turquoise wings burst through the back of Nula's blouse and she took off, narrowly missing Yaron's flames.

But not the ceiling.

She fell to the ground, clutching her head. Lirome, now in skin form, rushed to her side, reaching out to calm her.

<You have chosen very poorly, Tiers. It will be your end as well as hers—>

Yaron's words garbled as Tiers grabbed his head and twisted with all his strength, snapping his neck and throat.

At the sound, a hard, hollow relief filled Tiers. Yaron would never haunt him again.

It was done.

He removed his hands from the head of his former fleetwing. Yaron's body fell to the ground, lifeless.

<The poor choice, and the end, were yours.>

Footsteps echoed down the corridor behind him. He ignored them, instead walking slowly over to Nula, each step bringing fresh pain from the wounds inflicted by Yaron. Hopefully, Lirome's sister wouldn't mind another healing session. At this point, the arcs of electricity would be a kindness compared to the agony in his throat and gut.

"Dragon! You're under arrest. Explain this."

Likely some well-meaning human law enforcement officer. Someone who needed answers.

Tiers would give them. But that didn't mean he had to turn around.

"There are the two rogue dragons from the Pinnacle that Nula Thredsing promised the council."

He fell to his knees and took his embermate in his arms, utterly spent.

CHAPTER TWENTY

BLOOD AND ICE splattered her arms. Dank, shadowy mud sucked at her legs, pulling her deeper and deeper into the mire.

She tried to scream. Tried to fight her way out. But each action made her sink deeper.

A figure descended from above her. Hope lit within her. A friend?

As it came closer, she could see it wasn't a person. The falling shape separated into two objects. One of them fell to the mud in the distance, an oblong shape with stalky limbs.

The other hit the mire in front of her, where she had now sunk up to her chest.

A human-shaped head stared up at her, its face twisted in a hideous grimace.

Yaron Flamestriker.

Nula lurched up in bed, her back soaked in sweat. Her scarf had fallen to her shoulders, and she clutched the blankets, staring into the dark room around her. A room that was warm and open, with no traces of mud, blood, or corpses falling from the sky.

Something touched her shoulder. She flinched, turning toward the source. Tiers stared back at her, his expression pained and sheepish, his dark hair ruffled all over his head.

<I'm sorry.> He sighed. <That was … me.>

<You? You mean … it was your nightmare?>

He grimaced. <Yes.>

Nula turned to face him, the memory of the nightmare replaced by questions. <Is it normal for embermates to see each other's dreams? Will that always happen?>

Tiers sighed. <I don't know. We've only been heart-bound for a day and a night.> He leaned back against the cushioned headboard, rubbing his eyes. <I'll ask Zephryn tomorrow. At the least, he could offer more information from his many books.>

<Good idea. We should learn as much as possible so we know how to properly deal with the embermate bond and everything associated with it.>

Tiers gave a weak nod, his shoulders slouching. <You can try to sleep more, if you wish.>

<You can't?>

<I think I might be done for the night.>

Deep weariness and sorrow filled her through their bond, breaking through the haze of sleep. Nula could have swallowed her tongue. Of course he was having trouble sleeping. He had just killed someone who had been his closest friend for years. Killed him with his bare hands.

Nula scooted closer to him, taking his hand in hers. <It only happened a day ago. No one would recover quickly from that.>

<Not even you?> He raised his eyebrows.

She laughed shortly. <After I watched Dayevid's execution, I didn't sleep well for weeks.>

<What did you do?>

Nula shrugged. <I worked until I passed out. Or I'd get really drunk.> She paused, reluctant to share more, but compelled by the weight of her past. <Sometimes, I'd go to a club and find some distraction in someone else's arms. You know. Sex.>

His golden eyes twinkled. <I do understand human euphemisms. But I appreciate the effort to clarify. I still don't understand why you choose not to speak plainly.>

<Euphemisms are the language of human politics. Foolish, but very necessary for my line of work.>

She leaned her head on his shoulder, enjoying the quiet rhythm of their two hearts beating as one. Grateful for the relief of their embermate bond. Grateful that the wings that had erupted from her back during the fight with Jylle had disappeared soon after, vanishing into the Nether, the place Between that shifters were innately connected with, and that she still had no idea how to access.

Eventually, wings might be nice. Right now, she had enough to deal with.

Finally, Tiers spoke. <So what helped you to sleep?>

<Zilpath's temple, believe it or not.>

<You're religious?>

Nula shrugged. <I can see potential futures, what brings people value, and what increases their value. It means there must be a bigger plan I'm getting glimpses of. I'm not sure I agree with all the details of the Four Corners religion, but I found peace in surrendering to a Greater Power and acknowledging that there had to be a reason for everything. I still go there, occasionally.>

Tiers wrapped an arm around her, his fingers tracing the scales on her shoulder. <I can understand that. I don't hold with everything Lirome says about magic and spirit, but what his sister did, what I did with the magical alarms … it was different. Perhaps sometime I'll go with you.>

<I'd like that.> Nula tsked. <So would Zilpath. Beware. She'll

immediately begin a campaign for a temple wedding ceremony.>

<I thought you had accepted that we were married. And that we would just petition for humans to accept it as well and sign any necessary documents.>

<Yes, but she takes the Four Corners very seriously, and since I've resigned myself to a few things about it, she … well, I think it would make her happy.> Nula sighed. <Speaking of ceremony, what time is it?>

Tiers eased away from her to check the timepiece. <We have to get up in a half hour.>

Nula yawned. <Well, there's little point in going to sleep. I think we should take a bath.>

<Oh, should we?>

<Yes. I'm sweaty from the nightmare, and you probably are as well. And we might find other ways to spend the extra time.> She smiled, trailing her fingers across his shoulder and down his chest. She leaned in close enough to nip his ear and whisper, "Of course, if you're afraid of a little water, I suppose you don't need to partake."

His elegant face stretched into a grin as he pulled her close. "I think I can cope in this situation." His hands traveled down her torso, lingering on her scales, still present and sensitive to his touch. "After all, we should present a united front at the ceremony. For political reasons, naturally."

"Naturally."

She pressed her mouth to his, tasting his irresistible heat and fire. He returned her kiss fiercely, lifting her up in his arms and carrying her off to the bathroom.

All the better. A much wiser use of their energy. It even conserved water.

Then, all rational thoughts left her mind.

Her clipse-mirror was beeping.

Nula glanced at it, annoyance filling her. Her dress for her presentation as grand countess had been freshly ironed. Sitting down too long could cause wrinkles.

The clipse-mirror continued its shrill chirp.

"Very well. Please be someone important."

She stalked over and pressed her hand to the mirror screen. An image of a dragon in skin form appeared, her brown hair loose and her amber eyes weary.

"Kesia?" Nula found a chair, her irritation partly forgotten. "What is it?"

"I just wanted to wish you congratulations on your presentation as grand countess." Kesia's delicate brow wrinkled. "That's something humans do, right? Well-wish? I've seen them do it."

"Yes, humans do that." After knowing Tiers, Nula was discovering that Kesia and Zephryn's ignorance of human customs wasn't merely a dragon thing. It was the result of their imprisonment and upbringing under the cruel Pinnacle. Kesia had shown strong interest in engaging with other cultures, unlike her embermate, Zephryn. "Thank you. I'm glad the day has finally come. I had no doubt it would, even when I was lying on a table being struck with electricity from a unicorn."

A smile played at Kesia's lips, proving she'd caught Nula's dry humor. She had always been better at that than Zephryn. "I can't wait to read that report! Lirome and Maira sound like interesting people."

Nula noticed the melancholy in the dragon's voice. Something to think about later. "'Interesting' is a good word for them. You'll have an opportunity to meet them soon. They're going to the Scepter of Knowledge as reinforcements for the Lawless."

Along with the cat-dragon, who had scarcely left Maira's side since she had been rescued. But Kesia could discover that fact in her own time.

"Oh?" The dragon sat up, staring at Nula intently. "Why?"

Nula grimaced. "Terms of their cooperation, actually, as well as payment for their assistance this past week. Lirome Ukerys has vital information on the downfall of Elotrin and how it is currently affecting Sekastra and the wartime issues, more information than he has previously given to the heads of the Lawless." Smart unicorn, piecing out information as a negotiation tool. "He's only willing to speak with the heir to the dragon throne. It's some vow he made." Kesia nodded, and Nula continued. "His sister, Maira, is trying to find someone named Tyrius Stormsong. They have some sort of strong bond. From what I've learned from other sources, he might be a dangerous individual."

Alarm tightened the dragon's face. "She thinks she'll find him in the Scepter of Knowledge? What kind of bond do they have?"

"She refuses to explain it, but I overheard conversation that Tyrius is her chief mate. So some kind of relationship is involved, and those always complicate things. Also, Tiers and I have noticed that when the unicorns get to a certain heightened state, their eyes flash blood red."

Kesia leaned forward. "Blood red? Are there any other signs? Maybe a scent?"

"Maybe … sulfur? Maybe not. Nothing strong enough for me to notice." Nula shrugged. "They're hiding something. Something very dangerous. They've been through darkness, and it shows.

Something tells me the higher-ups in the Lawless know a lot more than they are saying." Nula shrugged. "But during the short time the unicorns were here, they cared for the wounded among the Lawless. Even Maira, and she's still recovering. Oh, and they both spent time in the Four Corners temple."

"Religious piety and selfless healing of others. Dangerous secrets. Just what we need. More uncertainties. More difficulties." Kesia sighed, slouching in her seat. "At least they will be new people."

"I have no doubt you and Zephryn can handle it together. Embermate bonds are wonderful like that." Nula smiled slyly. "I'm certainly not complaining."

Kesia shrugged. "Oh, our bond is good. He's just busy doing research. The Scepter of Knowledge has quite a few libraries, and Zephryn is overwhelmed by everything."

"You aren't helping him?"

"I do sometimes, but I get bored. When we were imprisoned, we talked about studying side by side for hours. But now that we have the chance to do so, I lose interest before he does." She paused, then winked, her expression turning lighter. "It's not bad. It's just something new to figure out. Of course, Zephryn and I are in constant connection with each other, so it isn't like I'm actually away from him when I'm exploring. And I go with Shance sometimes. I'm trying to convince him to stop having sex with random women. It never makes him happier in the long run. He should find someone and commit."

"It seems like he's looking, in his own way." Nula tsked. "But the day Windkeeper settles down is the day dragons refuse to fly."

Kesia chuckled. "Maybe."

Nula glanced at the timepiece. "Kesia, I need to go."

"All right."

The clipse-mirror went blank. Nula shook her head. The dragon still hadn't caught on to human leave-takings. It was just as well. They were pointless.

Nula stood, smoothed down the folds of her silver gown, and left her dressing room to meet Tiers.

He stood waiting in the hall in a finely-tailored black suit with a silver waistcoat. They'd decided on the colors after determining that silver would set off his golden scales and her turquoise ones. Nula had managed to retract her wings but still hadn't mastered hiding her scales, and Tiers was perfectly willing to show his own in support. She couldn't argue with how they looked against his tawny skin. In fact, part of her wanted to go find an empty room and explore each part of him again.

<You were almost late.> His lips twitched as he offered her his arm.

<Kesia wanted to chat. It gave me a chance to tell her about the two new arrivals to the Scepter of Knowledge.>

Tiers escorted her outside. <I'm still not certain that sending Maira and Lirome was a wise idea. We know so little about them or this Tyrius Stormsong they are concerned about.>

<Wise or not, it's the one decision everyone could agree to. War makes strange bedfellows, and much of the country is still in conflict.> Nula straightened his cravat. <They're all capable—dragons, unicorns, and humans alike. I'm sure they can manage.>

<Like we managed?>

<Exactly.>

He guided her to the groundcar that waited by the curb. "After you, Grand Countess Nula Thredsing."

She grinned and entered the car.

A cat-dragon blinked at her from the middle seat. Surprise

filled Nula, along with a flicker of delight.

"Ah, did you decide to view the ceremony before joining the unicorns?"

Freckles curled up on the seat and flicked his tail.

Apparently so.

Well, if the council could get used to a half-dragon, ex-double agent grand countess, then they could adapt to a cat-dragon attending the reconciliation ceremony. A thrill rose within her. Nula would formally receive her seat on the Scepter of Commerce council. Accompanied by her dragon spy husband.

Yes, the future held mysterious unicorns and ominous workings of the Curious Intrigue. Nula and Tiers needed use Tiers's espionage contacts to learn if the SPU had, in fact, been part of a plot to ensure that Talents never emerged within individuals. Then, there was the work of integrating dragons into the Scepter of Commerce, as well as the forthcoming execution of her parents. Legal executions required too much paperwork.

She glanced over at Tiers, who sat on the other side of the ground car. His golden eyes fixed on hers. She sensed his heart beating in time with hers, his keen awareness of the pain she hid from so much of the world.

Then he reached out and took her hand, his warmth reminding her that she would never again face the future alone.

And that was enough.

Sign up for Janeen Ippolito's newsletter and get exclusive bonus content from The Ironfire Legacy series, plus monthly giveaways, book recommendations, and excerpts:

Thank you for reading!

The Ironfire Legacy Series:
Outlaw of Smoke
Scion of Scales
Captain of Storms

About the Author

Janeen Ippolito believes you should own your unique words—and make them awesome! She's a multi-published author of bestselling fiction, nonfiction, and poetry. She's also an experienced book editor and marketing strategist. In her spare time, she helps her missionary husband with his youth swordfighting ministry, indulges her foodie ambitions, reads whatever books she feels like, and explores a slew of random hobbies. Her life goals include traveling to Antarctica and riding a camel while wearing a party hat. This extrovert loves to connect, so join her on social media or at janeenippolito.com

ACKNOWLEDGEMENTS

To the real Maker of All, whom I owe every breath to.

Much love to my husband, Stephen Ippolito, who continues to be patient with me ignoring him to write fantasy worlds—and then reads my books!

Shout-out to alpha readers Sarah Delena White, Bethany Jennings, and Hannah Keeler for your encouragement along the first draft journey, even when I was sure everything was DOOMED (a stage in my writing process every time).

Thanks to beta readers Claire Banschbach, Kate Allen, Rachel Harbour, and H. L. Burke for the valuable feedback!

Especial thanks to Sarah Delena White and Sarah Bowen for on-call opinions on how to make the lives of specific characters way worse (and then make them better).

Major appreciation to Sarah McConahy for continuing to put up with me and edit my stuff.

Much thanks to Christian Bentulan for another gorgeous cover!

Shout-out to The Marvelous Misfits, the best reader group an author could have. Y'all rock!

www.ingramcontent.com/pod-product-compliance
Lightning Source LLC
Chambersburg PA
CBHW030344180626
46812CB00007B/2753
* 9 7 8 1 9 4 8 8 9 6 5 6 6 *